SINS OF THE FATHER

The Father Barrett Files #2

JAMIE MASON

ROUGH
EDGES
PRESS

Rough Edges Press
An Imprint of Wolfpack Publishing
5130 S. Fort Apache Rd. 215-380
Las Vegas, NV 89148

roughedgespress.com

Paperback ISBN 978-1-68549-148-2
eBook ISBN 978-1-68549-147-5
LCCN 2022942899

SINS OF THE FATHER

"A beast does not know that he is a beast, and the nearer a man gets to being a beast, the less he knows it."

– George MacDonald

Asshole

IT WAS Mrs. Anderson who gave Barrett the fucking dog.

"Now father, you *will* make sure Princess Woogums gets her num-nums, won't you?" Edith Anderson paused halfway down the rectory corridor to gaze back at the miniature bulldog slumped in the kitchen doorway. "We've been together so long. Ever since Edgar died…"

"Now, mum." Homer Anderson, Edith's twenty-something son, laid a hand on her arm. "Dad died back in 2008. And we got—ah—*Princess* Woogums last year. Remember?" He winked at Barrett.

"Oh?" She frowned. "Edgar's dead? Really?"

Barrett gritted his teeth behind the vapid grin he'd been wearing for the past eight weeks as he watched Edith Anderson plunge headlong into dementia. He had gotten to know Princess Woogums quite well—well enough to be acquainted with the bulldog's foul nature, incontinence, slobbering and tendency to bark at empty space for no apparent reason. Princess Woogums was not far behind Mrs. Anderson in the dementia department.

Princess Woogums was also male.

"Don't you worry, Mrs. Anderson." Barrett spoke patiently. "I'll take wonderful care of, um, *Princess Woogums*. I'll see to it *she* finds a good forever home." He glared at the wrinkly mess on the kitchen threshold decked out with a garish pink ribbon as it sat farting and slobbering on itself. "Don't you worry about a thing."

"You're sure it's not an imposition?" Mrs. Anderson twisted against her son's grasp and craned toward Barrett, elongating the encounter.

Perhaps she senses she's going to the nuthatch, Barrett thought. *She's trying to drag it out.* He felt a twinge of compassion for her, as a priest should. But not for long.

I'm not really that kind of priest, he reminded himself.

Mostly he just wanted a cigarette. And a drink.

He followed the Andersons out of the parish house to the sidewalk. To his surprise, Princess Woogums shambled after them, making little grunts of effort. Barrett helped steady Edith Anderson as she marched toward Homer's SUV. The dog, meanwhile, deposited himself on his butt on the lawn, raised one leg and proceeded to lick his prodigious testicles.

"Take care, sweet little girl," crooned Mrs. Anderson. "Mommy will miss you! You be good for Father Barrett now. And who knows?" She grinned mischievously. "Perhaps *he'll* become your forever home!"

"Don't know that my housekeeper will go for it," Barrett said mildly, enumerating ways he could dispose of Princess Woogums. All of them humane, of course.

Well…most of them…

He snapped out of it. "Mrs. Anderson…" He extended a hand. "God bless and take care in your journey. I'll stop by when I next come through Parksville. You betchya."

"Parksville?" Mrs. Anderson snorted. "We're going to Disneyland! C'mon, Homer. Let's blow this popsicle stand!"

She leapt into the passenger seat of the SUV and slammed the door.

Homer sighed. "Father, I can't thank you enough. You've been incredibly helpful."

"No worries, Homer." Barrett fished out cigarettes and lit one. "Least I could do after you let me take a look at that surveillance videotape last November. It helped me and Sergeant Lewis finally locate Jackie, thank God. Besides, I like your mum. She's good people."

"God bless you, father."

"You too, Homer. See you Sunday."

Barrett watched the SUV pull away and remained smoking by the curb long after they vanished.

Pastoral care had never been his thing. But he'd extended himself for Homer and his mom and surprised himself by liking it more than he expected. Having spent most of his years in the priesthood doing solitary work, running a parish and actually becoming *involved* in other people's lives felt...

Weird.

Behind him, the dog sneezed. Barrett felt the warm, wet impact of something on his ankle.

"Okay." He clenched his teeth, turned and ground his cigarette out under foot. "First things first: you are *not* a bitch. You are a *male* dog and you are hereby no longer called Princess-fucking-Woogums." Barrett reached down and undid the ribbon from around the beast's neck. "From henceforth your name will be—"

The dog sneezed again, leaning forward over Barrett's shoe as he did so. A pint of moist phlegm enveloped Barrett's shoe, warming his foot in its sock.

"Asshole!"

The dog looked up.

"Okay! It's settled, then!" Barrett fished out a hand-kerchief and knelt. "From henceforth you are Asshole. We'll think up another name when we find some gullible mark to adopt you. But until then your name is Asshole. Got it?" Barrett finished scrubbing himself and stood. "C'mon, Asshole. Time for a drink."

Asshole shambled after Barrett as he went back into the kitchen, opened the cupboard above the sink and hauled down a box of red wine. The box was pleasantly heavy, difficult to balance yet full of the promise of not having to go out for refills again later that day. Barrett lowered it to the counter, fished a mug from the dish drainer and spritzed himself a foamy serving from the plastic spigot.

"You see, Asshole..." Barrett toasted the dog. "I wasn't always the beneficent, charismatic, people-oriented parish priest you see before you. No, for the longest time I worked for the Curia. That's *right*. The Vatican itself! I was a Papal investigator. A wolf of the Inquisition. I tracked down pedophile priests and other wrongdoers for the Congregation of the Doctrine of the Faith. What do you think of that?"

Asshole yawned.

"Well, you would say that, wouldn't you, you ungrateful little shit." Barrett gulped more wine, bent to the spigot and topped it up. "Dumb, too. You don't recognize what a career achievement that signifies. The trust, Asshole. The *trust*. Of the Curia! The very mind and soul of the Roman Cath... Oh, really? Do you have to do that?"

Asshole, who had raised a leg to relieve himself,

peered guiltily back over his shoulder then slowly lowered it to the floor.

"Good Asshole! We'll teach you about where to poop and piddle. But for now it's important that you realize that you are sharing a home with a member of the Society of Jesus, a man who once... Hey. *Hey!*"

Asshole had lifted his leg again. Urine spread in a large elliptical puddle around the kitchen table. Asshole finished, farted, then shambled over to the doorway where he flung himself down and promptly fell asleep.

Barrett blinked.

That little...FUCKER!

The temptation was there to take a running kick at the thing, but Christian charity prevailed. He couldn't kick an innocent creature whose only crime was being sloppy and stupid. Violence was to be held in reserve and delivered unto the deserving. As Barrett had done in the past. Had done. And *still* could. Concealed in the drawer by the fridge was a Glock 19 engraved with the Papal arms and registered as a weapon with the Vatican armory of the Swiss Guard. Only Swiss Guardsmen and Papal special investigators carried such firearms—this one being a relic of his former life. Barrett had fired that gun his during his decade with the Curia...

But those were memories for another day. For *now* he had this fucking dog to consider—this animal that pissed all over things and slept in doorways.

"You need a collar." Barrett set down his glass and dug through a drawer. "God forbid you try to escape and somehow end up outside. We don't have a dog catcher in Fulton but you might get picked up by Walton, the Conservation officer. Wouldn't want him thinking you were some feral stray that wandered in from the forest. Here."

Barrett withdrew a worn silver crucifix on a leather thong which had mysteriously ended up in the spoon drawer. Barrett had moved it back and forth for months while digging for coffee spoons without ever thinking much about it until now.

"Now...sit up. Hey! Asshole!" Barrett knelt, snapping his fingers until the dog lurched completely upright. He bent and tied the crucifix around its neck. "There. Now if you get out, people will know where to return you. *Dominus vobiscum.* Congratulations, you're Catholic."

Asshole peered at Barrett for a long moment, blinked and fell back to sleep.

"Now that you've christened the rectory kitchen..." He took a hard swallow of red, grabbed a sponge and some paper towels and fell to mopping up the puddle. He was just finishing up and washing his hands when the phone rang.

No rest for the wicked... He picked up and set the receiver between shoulder and chin as he dried his hands on a dishtowel.

"St. Michael's and St. Joan's Catholic Church. Father Barrett speaking. How may I help you?"

"Father? Father Michael Barrett?" asked a woman's voice.

"Speaking." Barrett hoisted his mug, finished the contents and lit a cigarette.

"Oh, thank goodness. Father, I'm calling from Fulton District Hospital. Arnold McLellan is here. His family is asking to see you."

Barrett's insides flushed cold. He knew what this meant.

"I'll be there shortly." He checked his watch.

"Thank you, Father." The nurse hung up.

Barrett sighed and lowered the receiver to the cradle.

"Richest man in Fulton," he muttered. "About to learn that you can't take it with you."

Stepping over the sleeping dog, he left the kitchen and began gathering the items to administer Last Rites.

———

BARRETT PULLED out of the church parking lot and made for the highway. When the on-ramp appeared, he gunned the accelerator, bulleting the Hyundai forward into the quiet grey morning like Steve McQueen, counting on the fact that there was no one in sight. Arnold McLellan wasn't Barrett's favorite person, or even a regular parishioner, but the two had come into contact during the final stages of McLellan's long, slow, torturous surrender to cancer. Barrett wanted to get there before McLellan went—mostly for the sake of the hospital staff. He was calculating how many minutes he was shaving off when the morning behind him exploded in a blare of noise and blue light. Barrett saw red flash in the rearview, heard the whoop of the siren, slowed and pulled to the shoulder.

He checked his watch.

McLellan's life was ticking away.

Asshole, Cont'd

SERGEANT GAVIN LEWIS, RCMP took his time sauntering up to the Hyundai's driver side window. Once there, he bent and hooked an elbow over the edge of the open window and smirked knowingly at Barrett.

"On your way to an exorcism, padre?"

"No. I have to administer Last Rites to Arnold McLellan."

"Is that right?" Lewis drew in a sharp breath and stood upright. "At the hospital, is he? You been counselling with him?"

"I have. Gavin, I'm sorry for speeding. I'll pay the ticket."

"Nah." The cop flapped a hand. "But for Jesus sake, *slow down* in future. You're roaring through here like Mario Andretti. 'Course, I can see why. McLellan is…"

"He's at FDH, yeah."

"Okay." Lewis hooked his thumbs in his gun belt. "If McLellan's dying, that means there's a damn good chance his younger son Mark might be back. Or on his way back."

"Is that bad?"

"Very bad." Lewis made for his car. "I should be there just in case. Follow me."

"Right."

Barrett twisted the key in the ignition, waiting until Lewis had pulled out ahead of him. Once Barrett had closed the gap between them, the Mountie went Code Two, lights and sirens. For Barrett, it was like being back on the force in Toronto before joining the Jesuits—that weird, almost sexual mix of adrenalin and fear coursing through his brain and bowels during a high-speed chase. They blasted onto the highway, heading for the hospital.

————

THE HYUNDAI PULLED up behind the Crown Victoria parked in the ambulance bay. The charge nurse, seeing Barrett was clergy, said nothing about his chosen spot and just waved them both through. As they crossed the waiting area, Barrett noted the headline of the local paper someone had abandoned on a bench:

LOCAL FIRST NATIONS YOUTH MISSING

His gut tightened.

Provincial news had been filled with heavy coverage of the Highway of Tears disappearances and the ongoing national crisis involving missing and murdered Indigenous women. An unsatisfactory Parliamentary inquiry and the ongoing deterioration of First Nations' living conditions combined to ensure that very little improved on small reserves like the one near Fulton. The loss of another youth was something the local band, the Otter People, could ill afford. Barrett made a mental note to check in with the tribal Chief first chance he got.

A security guard conducted them to the small hospice wing, located at the quiet end of an otherwise deserted floor. A single clerk sat at the nurse's station, but otherwise the place was empty.

"Room Four." The guard pointed.

Inside, a figure lay prostrate on the bed, watched over by a towering presence. Barrett blinked into the gloom and recognized Tristan McLellan, Arnold's oldest son, looming in the half-light. Somehow the shadows seemed to fit the moment, so Barrett didn't touch the switch when he entered. He moved around to observe the form of Arnold McLellan, local entrepreneur, philanthropist, real estate magnate, financial baron, and all-round wheel of Fulton where he lay on his back, eyes closed, not long for this world.

McLellan owned a dozen businesses in town, half the property outside it and employed over a thousand people on the island (including Homer Anderson, Asshole's human ex-step-brother, who worked security at McLellan's big box retail). The death of such a man was bound to be complicated and, from what Barrett could see, imminent. Emaciated and dishevelled, his yellowing skin hollow and his eye-sockets sunken and dark, Arnold McLellan resembled a denizen of the walking dead. Barrett crossed himself.

"Tristan." Sergeant Lewis' gravelly whisper was loud in the still room. "Very sorry about this."

Tristan McLellan drew a measured breath of exasperation.

"Sergeant Lewis," he said quietly, "we're going to need security at the memorial service. My father, although a community benefactor, had enemies. Enemies which, even though he's dead—"

"I'm *not* dead!"

All three of them jumped. Arnold McLellan, ashen-cheeked and pale as snow, was suddenly peeling the oxygen mask from his face and sitting up, plainly annoyed. Barrett waved down a nurse in the corridor. A moment later, three came running and attended to the dying man.

"It happens," explained one as the other two straightened McLellan's bedclothes and fiddled with his monitors. "People in their final stages sometimes fade and return. It can be very dramatic. One moment they look like they're at death's door and the next day they're out taking a walk. The energy spikes and wanes very fast."

"Oh, and look!" McLellan shoved away one nurse's hand, jabbing a finger at Barrett. "They even sent for the priest! They must have *really* thought I was a goner! Couldn't wait to get rid of me eh, Tristan?"

"Father, don't be—"

"Don't be *what?*" McLellan flung his arms around like he was shooing away a cloud of gnats. The nurses fled. "Jesus Mickey Mouse! You think I don't know what goes through your minds? You, Lewis, are wondering about public bequests, aren't you? Foundation money? Donations to the town? Meanwhile you, Tristan—"

"Father, that's enough."

"*You're* thinking about grabbing the family assets and selling them all to finance your pipe dreams. Ha!" McLellan turned to Barrett. "And then there's you."

"Here I am." Barrett smiled uncomfortably. McLellan was, of course, dying. But Barrett didn't feel particularly sympathetic. He noticed that, at some point, the nurses had left. He couldn't really blame them. "So good to see you recovered, Mr. McLellan."

"How diplomatic of you," sneered McLellan. "All my life I've been surrounded by double-talk. Is that what I get in death, too? Jesus. Tristan? Go get your father a sandwich and a coke, will you? I'm starving."

"Mr. McLellan, I came because of Mark." Gavin Lewis stepped to the foot of the bed and addressed McLellan directly. "You don't suppose he'll be—"

"Back? That little son-of-a-bitch? No. In fact, I should write him out of the will entirely. I'll make arrangements to do that. And father? You and I need to talk funeral arrangements."

"Of course, Mr. McLellan." Barrett turned to Lewis. "I got this. I'll call you if the boy shows up."

"Right." Lewis nodded to McLellan and followed Tristan out of the room, pulling the door shut behind him. Barrett drew a chair up to the edge of the bed and produced his Bible.

"How do you feel, Mr. McLellan?"

McLellan's face took on a distant expression. "I think… I came very close there, father." The rich man's voice was suddenly soft, full of wonder. "Like as in right up close to the edge. Of dying. It was…"

"How was it, my son?"

Silence. Barrett sensed McLellan gathering the courage to ask his next question.

"Father. Do you believe in Hell?"

Barrett found himself wishing he'd paid more attention during those mandatory seminars on counselling. He bit the inside of one cheek, struggling to mask his discomfort and measure his response—no mean feat.

Asking a Vatican investigator if he believes in Hell is like asking a combat veteran if he believes in PTSD…

"Some modern theologians are questioning the existence of Hell as it's traditionally been presented," Barrett admitted. "Some of the remarks from the current pontiff point in that direction. No, Arnold. I think Hell is something we create for ourselves. In Catholicism, we believe the spirit exists in eternity so whatever we begin on Earth continues after our time here ends."

The color was coming back to McLellan's cheeks, and a twinkle lit his eye. "So, if I'm living a pretty good life here on Earth, then I'll continue to do that in heaven?" He smirked. "Is that what you're saying?"

"Well, yes and no…"

McLellan's face reddened. "Well then what *are* you saying, padre?"

"It's not like ancient Egypt, Arnold." Barrett fought down rising frustration, and a genuine desire to hit something. "We're not burying you in a gold-lined sarcophagus along with your chariot and horses and a retinue of household slaves. It doesn't work that way."

"Then how *does* it work?"

"You have to have lived a good life. You have to be a decent human being."

This gave McLellan pause. "I've…been a decent human. I've given a great deal of money to charity. Oh, sure. I've taken some, too. And I've been…difficult. With some people. But I haven't *murdered* anybody…"

"Arnold…" Barrett smiled tiredly. "God doesn't want to negotiate with you."

"Well, why the hell not?" McLellan sounded genuinely insulted. "I'm a good negotiator. I've earned my place at the table."

"*Whose* table?" Barrett kept his tone deliberately neutral. "You're at a point in your life where you should be putting some things into perspective, don't you think?

It's difficult but sometimes you have to let go of old ways of thinking."

"But *what am I, padre, if I'm not the sum total of what I've built in this lifetime?*"

"You're the sum total of what you've built in this lifetime. Only with*out* money or possessions. It's what you've built with your heart, with your relationships. That's the treasure you've laid up for yourself here on Earth."

"Well, there's my family."

"That's the most important."

"Tristan..." McLellan screwed up his face and punched the air. "That boy is *such* a disappointment. But he's the one I have left, you understand. The one who survived all the purges. All the expulsions from, ah, 'McLellan Island.'" He laughed softly. "But weak. He's weak, father."

"We're all weak. In the end."

"Hell of a time to mention it!"

"I think now is the perfect time to mention it. Like I said: time to be putting things into perspective."

"So you keep telling me..."

Barrett let the tempo of the conversation fade into a semi-uncomfortable silence. There was very little he could say to McLellan at this stage that would change his mind about salvation or redemption. Failing that, Barrett figured he could at least comfort the man. But McLellan didn't seem interested in being comforted.

"You never answered my question. About whether or not you believe in Hell, father."

"Yes, I believe in Hell."

"But you find it hard to talk about. I think I know why." The twinkle in the old man's eye was back. "I had you checked out, you know. Soon after you got here. Hired a guy. He looked into your background."

"Oh? What background is that?"

"With the Congregation of the Doctrine of the Faith."

Barrett's felt his insides lurch—a fact he managed to conceal by keeping his expression neutral and remaining perfectly still. He did not return the conversational volley, forcing McLellan to serve again.

"Is it true what they say about you, padre? That you put that bishop in the hospital? The one who was sexually molesting those kids?"

"Yes."

"Why?"

"*Why?*" Barrett curled his right fist. "Because he was a bad man. Because he'd been doing it for a long time and hurt a lot of kids very deeply. Some had even resorted to suicide. He was a destroyer of souls. He had to be made to answer. In the eyes of God and Law. We had to be seen to make him answer."

"So for you, there is justice at the end of it all. That's part of the package. You spoke of God. *And* Law. Alright then. That's what I want to understand. God's Law."

"Why? So you can bend it?" Barrett regretted the words the moment he spoke them.

"No. So I can make a *deal* with it."

Barrett's insides flushed cold.

"What *is* Hell, Father Barrett?" McLellan managed to push himself up on one elbow and meet the priest's gaze directly.

Barrett had had enough of McLellan for one day.

"Let me answer that question with one of my own. Which do you love more? Your sons or your riches?"

McLellan remained still for a long moment, considering. As the silence spun out second after second, becoming a full minute, Barrett was awash in disbelief.

He doesn't know the answer!

His cellphone rang. Cursing himself for not shutting it off, he answered curtly:

"Barrett."

"Father Barrett. There is a *dog* here."

"Ah." It was his housekeeper. "Miss Dolan. Yes, that dog will be staying with us for a while."

McLellan, overhearing this, gave a wry grin and a phlegmy chuckle.

"I see. And what, pray tell, is this dog's *name?*"

Barrett swallowed. "Ah...I don't know. I'm open to suggestions."

"Fine. We can discuss it when you return. Which you will want to do soon."

"Why is that?"

"Because father. The rectory has been broken into and some items stolen."

Miss Dolan

BARRETT DROVE BACK to the rectory at top speed, muttering darkly under his breath. He was furious at himself for allowing Miss Dolan to hen-peck him so, furious for being furious and furious for doing nothing about it.

Well, I could do something but…

It was complicated!

Miss Dolan had just appeared unannounced one day on the rectory doorstep, claiming to be the housekeeper. She apparently had ties to the archdiocese. Her brother-in-law had been interim parish priest at St. Mike's and St. Jo's prior to—and, for a time, briefly after—Barrett's arrival. And she possessed a weirdly compelling way of forcing conversations to go in whatever direction she wanted, usually against Barrett. Meaning that, if she had pull with the bishop, arguing with her could prove troublesome. So it was just easier, in some things, to let her have her way…

The ever-insufferable Miss Dolan!

She was waiting at the door when he pulled into the

rectory driveway. Barrett killed the Hyundai's engine and took his time getting out, avoiding her gaze, hoping she would just go away but of course she didn't. She didn't even *look* away, just kept standing on the threshold, glaring. Barrett slammed the door and stalked toward her, head down, hands reaching automatically for cigarettes before remembering the trouble that erupted last time he lit up in her presence.

Miss Dolan!

He wasn't even sure she had a first name.

"I've put your *dog* in the *garage*." She flicked a finger toward the closed garage door. "What a filthy, smelly, ill-tempered brute. I'll thank you to keep him away from me, father."

Barrett nodded, understanding. He suddenly felt a newfound fondness for Asshole.

"I must tell you, father." Miss Dolan raised her chin and glared down at Barrett over a nose that was as bony and emaciated as the rest of her. "I spent the first fifteen minutes of my shift today cleaning up the dog's feces. Feces, father! In a *rectory!* And if that isn't bad enough, the health hazard to *me* as your official housekeeper…"

"Oh, listen… If you need to move on and work somewhere else, I'll completely understand, Miss Dolan…"

"And abandon my post? Not on your life!"

Barrett's heart sank.

"But I must insist that if you plan on keeping that *brute* that you properly house-train and walk him regularly so he does not engage in a repeat performance! And purchase a box of disposable rubber gloves for me in case he does. Please and thank you very much."

Barrett's temples were starting to throb. "You said the place got broken into?"

"Yes." She flicked the hem of her skirt and turned. "Come along, father, and I'll show you."

Miss Dolan walked ahead, heels clacking in rectory hall as she led them through the first doorway on the left into a small laundry room. Barrett heard the broken glass crunching under her shoes before entering and seeing the jigsaw puzzle of translucent triangles splaying the tile.

"See? He broke the window and clambered in over the dryer." She pointed. "He left a footprint."

Barrett bent to examine the mealy smudge near the dryer top's edge. An incomplete print, but there was enough of the heel to tell the burglar had worn hiking boots.

"Interesting," he muttered.

"Filthy," grated Miss Dolan. "He couldn't even be bothered to wipe his boots before coming in."

"Most burglars don't, Miss Dolan."

"Of course! Because they're filthy degenerates. This one probably smokes marijuana."

"That's legal now, Miss Dolan."

She sniffed. "That doesn't make it *right*, father."

Barrett sighed. "So, what's missing?"

"Looks to be he started in your bedroom, father." Miss Dolan led them through the living room then down the hall to the bedroom. She paused primly on the threshold. "Top two drawers."

Barrett stepped over and examined the detritus of his sock and underwear drawers.

"He probably left fingerprints!" Miss Dolan averred. "You should call the police and have them dusted!"

"That's a great idea." Barrett sighed, gathering up some fallen socks. "We'll bring Sergeant Lewis down here with his fingerprint kit and cameras. Have him spend a few hours around my sock drawer, then another few writing a stack of match analysis requests. By the time they're couriered to Ottawa, opened and analyzed, we'll be decorating for Christmas."

"That's six months from now!"

"That's RCMP bureaucracy, Miss Dolan." Barrett walked down the hall to the bathroom. "Didn't you say something about…"

"The medicine cabinet, yes." She trailed after him. "It seems that our filthy, grubby thief helped himself to some of your personal items."

Barrett stepped onto white tile, noting that the cabinet was indeed standing open. A quick inventory tallied the loss: toothpaste, a bar of soap in its wrapper, a fresh toothbrush, and some dental floss.

"The rest is in the kitchen." Miss Dolan cast a critical eye at the tub and muttered, "That'll need a scrub."

Barrett went, Miss Dolan's spinster shoes clunking along behind him. He entered the kitchen, counting the items scattered at the foot of the fridge. Then he went to the sink and pulled down his box of wine from the overhead cupboard.

"He took some food and… Ah." Miss Dolan's eyes narrowed in ritual disapproval. "I see you're starting into the drink early, father."

"Our Lord drank, Miss Dolan."

"Son of God can drink as much he wants, father. Human beings, on the other hand…"

"And do you know *why* He drank, Miss Dolan?" Barrett, ignoring her, poured himself a mug of wine, gulped half and topped it up. "It was because of His job."

"Saving the world from sin?"

"No. Being a rabbi. That's a kind of priest. We do the same job, Miss Dolan. We're both priests. And do you know what God does for us priests? He lets us drink as a little reward for having to deal with the public."

"Are you comparing yourself to Our Lord, father?"

"No. Just His… My God! Lighten up, will ya'? I've had a hell of a day!"

"The burden is the glory, father!"

Barrett stomped to the garage entrance and let himself in, slamming the door behind him. Asshole sat alone beside the lawn mower, gazing at Barrett with a kind of droopy disappointment.

"Well." Barrett leaned against the wall and lit a cigarette. "Here we are."

Asshole rose, shambled over and took a seat at the priest's feet. He looked from Barrett to the kitchen door and back again.

"Miss Dolan is, ah… She's tightly wound. You shouldn't take it too… Jesus, am I talking to a dog?"

Asshole heaved a patient sigh.

"Yeah, well. You won't have to deal with her, Asshole. You'll just stay in the garage whenever she comes over. We'll fix you up a little doggy wet bar or something. Anyway. Just be cool for the next hour or so while Eva Braun in there does her thing."

And with that Barrett stooped and gingerly rubbed the dog's head. Asshole responded with a low growl.

"The feeling's mutual." Barrett straightened and crushed out his cigarette. "For now, you stay in the garage. Capiche?"

Asshole turned, farted and shambled away, his outsize testicles jostling between his delicate hind legs.

When Barrett returned to the kitchen, Miss Dolan had just finished wiping off and putting away the packages left strewn on the floor.

"Have you, ah, called the police yet, Miss Dolan?"

"I have not, father. That's a decision that should be taken by the clergy."

"I appreciate your deference." Barrett made for the phone.

"You know, father. This has happened before." Miss Dolan paused in her tidying. "Break-ins in the rectory, I mean."

"Oh?" Barrett had been parish priest for just over eight months. Evidently, Miss Dolan's tenure here predated his own.

"It was when my dear brother was acting priest for this parish." Miss Dolan held up a hand. "Now, I know father that you two didn't quite get along…"

"That's putting it mildly," Barrett muttered, topping up his wine. Dolan had briefly replaced Barrett back in November after spray-painting a death threat on the wall of the rectory. He had tried to pass it off as the work of the local Indian teenagers. To the best of his knowledge, Miss Dolan's brother was still on administrative leave.

"Yes." She took a seat at the kitchen table, her fingers tugging at the sponge she'd just wrung out over the sink. "It was last summer around this time. My brother was filling in after Father Keating had his nervous break-down. Now, you know that my brother is fond of collecting things…"

"You're referring to his hoarding?"

"Now, father, that's putting things in their most uncharitable light…"

"You're aware that when he was here, his record collection took up my entire bedroom? I had to go live in a motel."

"Well, that's as may be." She flapped a hand. "But he's a very kind and charitable soul, father, and I daresay you could profit by his example."

Barrett stifled a laugh behind a well-timed cough.

"In either case, my brother was here filling in. And he had his things with him, as he usually does. Well, he went for a walk to the store and came back. And do you know what he found?"

"Someone had pilfered a thousand or so of his eight-track cassette tapes?"

"No, father. He returned to find the front door open and clues indicating the place had been burgled. Muddy footprints, like the ones we noticed. And the same items taken."

Barrett raised his eyebrows. "Go on." This was getting interesting.

"A number of pairs of my brother's socks and under-wear were gone. And he buys his bathroom necessaries in bulk, so a half-dozen tubes of toothpaste were missing. Soap, shampoo, toilet paper."

"That's…*very* interesting." Barrett reflected. The last theft had occurred in the summertime.

"My brother did a little bit of digging, father. He didn't find anything conclusive, but there *is* mention in the church records of a similar break-in a few years before."

Barrett felt a headache piling on behind his eyes, as it usually did when he spent too much time around Miss Dolan. Still, he gathered his resolve and put on a brave face to thank her.

"I'll take all of that into consideration, Miss Dolan, thank you." Barrett produced his cigarettes and lit one. Miss Dolan wrinkled her nose and left.

He smiled as he watched her go. Lighting up was the surest way to get rid of her.

———

BARRETT HIKED across the lot to the church and attacked the pile of paperwork on his desk. He made progress for about half an hour before becoming distracted by thoughts of the break-in.

Who the hell breaks into a church rectory and steals the priest's underwear? Barrett stepped outside to smoke, studying the clouds. Perhaps he was dealing with some weird fetishist who had a vendetta against priests. Or...

Summer both times. It's obviously seasonal.

Barrett returned to his desk and called Gavin Lewis at the detachment. No answer so he left a detailed message on the answering machine. Then he decided to clear his head. It was time to take Asshole for a walk.

Ghost

IT WAS AN UNPLEASANTLY warm June day. In typical Vancouver Island summer fashion, the air was humid enough to produce an oppressive mugginess. Each step Barrett took felt like wading knee-deep through a bowl of warm soup. Asshole, on the other hand, seemed to thrive in the heat.

Figures, Barrett thought. Being irritating must be woven into the creature's DNA. *I bet he's indestructible, too. Damn mutt will probably outlive me.*

Barrett fumbled for cigarettes, jammed one in his mouth and did his best to light it while juggling Asshole's leash. Of course, the bulldog chose that exact moment to begin barking and lunging at empty space for no apparent reason—an uncharacteristically athletic performance of growling and leash-twisting. Barrett cursed, struggling to bring the dog to heel while lighting up but it was hopeless. At length, he gave up trying to smoke, stuffed his cigarettes and lighter away, and resumed stalking up the street behind his new pet.

Temporary new pet, he corrected himself.

They turned down a side street two blocks from the parish house. In contrast to the cracked and rain-worn sidewalks in most of Fulton, the curbs here were a fresh and bright gray. This wide, curving road that looped up a hill behind town had been recently cut and the sidewalks newly poured. Barrett, who had not explored this part of Fulton in the eight months he had been in town, recalled a story in the local paper about a new property development that was generating some controversy. What the hell was it called?

Spirit Ranch Estates, Barrett remembered. He topped the hill and stared at the empty streets and immaculate lawns of a nearly finished but not yet inhabited subdivision. The places here were downright upscale and suburban compared to the worn businesses and down-at-heel government housing that characterized every other part of Fulton. It was another of Arnold McLellan's innumerable business enterprises, which was enough to cause the locale to inspire a foul taste in Barrett's mouth.

That man's got his tentacles into every money-making enterprise in town, he thought. No wonder there was friction between the two brothers, especially now when inheritance and such were in play. There was plenty at stake.

The road curved around a residential city block inset with model homes. Barrett couldn't imagine the business argument for placing modern, ranch-style homes replete with bay windows and well-groomed lawns out here in the wilderness between Gold River and Campbell River. *Unless they're thinking of selling Fulton as an attractive bedroom community,* Barrett thought. A bold move, but one that pervasive rural poverty, a fentanyl crisis and surging petty crime might make difficult. But given the magic of modern marketing, anything was possible.

Look at these places, he thought, wandering past stucco façades and thigh-high faux-ranch fencing of artisanal worn wood. The empty dwellings had the ghost-town feel of movie sets. So it was some relief when Barrett spied signs of life ahead.

Two men were standing and chatting on the sidewalk before a partially-completed ranch home. Barrett recognized the truck parked nearby as belonging to Adam Walton, Fulton's Conservation Service officer who shared office space with Gavin Lewis in the town's storefront police detachment. The CO was in uniform, standing with his back to Barrett and talking to someone the priest didn't recognize.

"Hey, padre." Walton turned when he heard Barrett's approaching footsteps, shading his eyes against the sun. "Got yourself a friend, I see."

"Yeah. Say. Either one of you guys interested in owning a dog?" Barrett pasted a phony smile in place as he stopped. Asshole took that opportunity to fart as he slumped into a sitting position. Now that the mutt was stationary, Barrett took advantage of the chance to light that cigarette he'd been craving.

"A dog?" Walton cast the mutt a skeptical look. "That ain't much of a dog there, padre…"

Asshole glanced sharply at Walton, as if understanding the insult, then very deliberately lifted his leg and began licking his crotch.

"How about you?" Barrett turned to the other man, a thirty-something guy in a ballcap and work shirt. "I don't believe we've met. I'm Father Michael Barrett."

"Max." The guy offered a tentative grin and a hand. "Max Simpson. I'm the property caretaker here at Spirit Ranch."

"Nice to meet you. Might you, ah…" Barrett coaxed

Asshole forward. "Might you consider adopting this wonderful animal?"

"Already got one, thanks." Max cast a pitying glance Asshole's way. "Doberman. He'd eat that little critter alive."

Damn! It seemed to Barrett like he would be stuck with Asshole forever.

"So what brings you out thisaway, Officer Walton?"

"Guarding a crime scene for Gavin until he can get here." Barrett knew the RCMP sergeant and CO routinely assisted each other in this way. "Max discovered something in this half-built house. You know those missing native kids?"

"Kids?" Barrett recalled the newspaper he'd spotted in the hospital waiting room on his way to visit McLellan. "I thought there was only one."

"Nope." Walton shook his head. "We've had our second disappearance in a month. A girl. Max was out cleaning up when he found her shoes and backpack."

"Really." Barrett raised his eyebrows. "Mind if I take a look?"

"Sure. Come on." Walton led them across the lawn to the house. To Max, he said: "Our local padre is an ex-police officer. Toronto, wasn't it?"

"Six years general patrol duty," Barrett replied. "Spent a lot of time in the inner city."

"Well, so what do you make of this?" Walton paused at the edge of the house's foundation and pointed downward.

The space was obviously intended to be a basement. Barrett saw cinderblock walls surrounding a concrete floor. A wooden staircase had already been built in anticipation of the walls and door that would go up around it. In the center was a bright pink Hello Kitty backpack.

Barrett noted it had been opened. A red sweater, child's size, spilled out of the zippered mouth. On the floor beside it was a pair of black sneakers with the laces untied.

"Interesting." Barrett narrowed his eyes. "The kid was undressed by an adult."

Walton raised his eyebrows. "Why do you say that?"

"Kids tend to kick off their shoes. Unlacing is too time-consuming. Also, that sweater? The one poking out of the backpack? That was being stuffed in, not pulled out."

"Oh?"

"See how the arms are tucked together?" Barrett mimed a folding gesture with his two hands. "He was intending to take it all with him when he was suddenly interrupted. So he grabbed the kid and left the bag half-packed."

Walton nodded. "I see it," he said, then looked up. Barrett followed his gaze to the curb where a van was approaching, one of those family SUV-type models. Instead of a soccer mom behind the wheel, a squat, dark First Nations woman navigated the unnamed streets of the Spirit Ranch development. In the passenger seat sat a man Barrett recognized instantly.

"Here comes the Chief," he said.

"I called him," Max said. "Soon as I found that. Called the police and the tribe."

Barrett watched as the van pulled up curbside and the door opened. As usual, the Chief was dressed in a green ballcap, shorts and sandals. Stooped and slightly portly, he looked like your average senior citizen, except that Barrett knew better. Despite appearances, the Chief possessed all the shrewdness and political savvy of an Atlantic City mob boss. He stepped to the ground, moving with his usual slow, shuffling gait. He turned and spoke to the woman behind the wheel. The van glided away as the Chief crossed the yard of the unfinished home and peered into the basement.

"Yep." He tugged off his ballcap and smoothed his thinning black hair before replacing the cap on his head. "That belongs to Sabrina. I recognize the shoes and sweater. And that's her Hello Kitty backpack."

Walton stepped forward. "Thank you, Chief. Sergeant Lewis is on his way right now. He's been working the other missing child case. But we're going to get right on this one, too. Don't you worry."

"I do worry, Officer Walton." The Chief's soft, kindly tone made these words all the more powerful. "My people's children are going missing. Like those women on that highway over on the mainland. The Highway of Tears, they're calling it. The cops there aren't doing shit about it."

Walton drew in a sharp breath. "Chief, you know where Gavin and I stand. With you guys. Sir, we're going to move hell and Earth to get your children back to you. I promise."

"Me, too," said Barrett. "The church will offer any help you need."

This made the old man smile. "Hello, Father Barrett. It's good to see you here."

"Chief, I'm so sorry…"

The old man was shaking his head now. Barrett could tell he was holding back tears of anger. "Is it because they hate Indian people? I don't know. But if it is, then I wouldn't mind so much them coming after me. I'll give them my phone number. They can come get me anytime. But to go after our children. *Anybody's* children! Father, why would they *do* that?"

"Evil. Plain and simple." Barrett's jaw firmed. He saw a suggestion of discomfort cross the faces of the other two men present, but Barrett didn't care. This was spiritual counselling time. And he knew the Chief to be a God man. "It's very fashionable these days to dismiss words like good and evil. But that's only by people who don't understand suffering."

"Indian people understand suffering, father."

"I know you do, Chief."

After speaking briefly with Walton, Max nodded and left. Barrett watched him go, striding across the yard of a finished unit and crossing it to disappear behind the house. Max probably had an office somewhere—probably a construction trailer. Given the development's suspension in litigation limbo, there probably wasn't a whole hell of a lot for the man to do.

"You know this is Indian land?" the Chief asked.

"No." Barrett was surprised. "It's not part of your reserve, is it?"

"It used to be. But old Arnold McLellan has other ideas." The Chief smiled. "I hear he's in the hospital now. I don't wish him harm. But a man like that ends up hurting himself more than he ever hurts others."

Barrett thought back to the bad blood between Tristan and Mark McLellan and reckoned the Chief was probably right.

"Father, may I ask you a personal question?"

"Of course, Chief. Anything."

"I wasn't snooping, but people talk. You hear things, you know?" The old man smiled sadly. "Is it true that you used to be an investigator for the church?"

"Yes." Barrett exhaled slowly, surprised at the unease he suddenly felt. "I was an investigator for the Congregation of the Doctrine of the Faith. The Inquisition, basically. I investigated personal and professional misconduct on the part of priests."

"I heard that you attacked one of them. One of the priests who sexually abused children. The man was a bishop. You put him in hospital."

"Yeah." Barrett's jaw firmed. "You see, when you chase down pedophiles long enough, something snaps inside you. After years of being impartial and professional, I just…couldn't anymore. I snapped. Went after him with a baseball bat. Smashed him up pretty good. He required multiple surgeries."

"Do you regret it?"

"My only regret is that I didn't kill the son-of-a-bitch."

The Chief nodded. "Well as far as I am concerned, father, you can do the same to whoever is taking our kids. I don't condone violence, but I wouldn't object, if you catch my drift."

"I think I do."

A white RCMP Crown Victoria turned a distant corner and drove toward them. Barrett could tell even from a distance that Lewis was burnt out. The Mountie drove very slowly, and with unusual care. Pursuing a missing child investigation while attending to all his routine daily duties was taking a toll on him. The lawman parked at the curb and got out, almost as stiffly as the Chief had. He came over with purpose in his gait.

"I've just come from Marianne Joe's place out by the river. We're continuing to run down every lead we have on Jason's disappearance. A few new clues have surfaced. We're making progress for you."

"Thank you, Gavin."

Lewis looked into the half-finished basement. "That Sabrina's stuff?"

"It is."

"Where's Max?" Lewis cast around.

"He took a powder," said Walton. "Need him?"

"Yeah. Run him down for me, would you Adam? I'll get the evidence collection kit from the car."

"Check." Walton jumped into his vehicle and went looking for the caretaker.

Lewis touched Barrett's arm. "Padre. Give me a hand with the evidence kit?"

"Sure."

Squatch

"LISTEN, PADRE...I COULD USE A HAND," said Lewis, stepping around to the Crown Vic's trunk and fumbling keys from his pocket.

"Whoa. Wait." Barrett held up his hands. "Are we talking more fun and games with criminal investigations? Because that last one with the bikers…"

"I need *help* here, Mike." Barrett could hear and see the desperation in Lewis' voice and eyes. "I got two missing Native kids. And there's already plenty of bad blood between the rez and the municipality because of McLellan's Folly, here." He waved a hand, encompassing all the houses, completed and incomplete, within view. "Now that the old bastard's dying, hopefully it can be settled in estate litigation. But meanwhile, I'm burning the candle at both ends and being run ragged. You're a trained investigator. Gimme a hand here."

"Fine." Barrett wrapped Asshole's leash around his wrist and crossed his arms. "But I want a damn raise. Last time, I got constable's pay. I'm worth more than that."

"Agreed." Lewis was nodding. "I had to make sure you had the chops. But you deserve a raise. Let's say... sergeant's pay. Same as mine. For the duration. Until we find these kids."

Barrett immediately felt ashamed. Here were Native kids getting kidnapped and he was concerned about his consulting fees. But then he reminded himself this was not just about them, but also about setting boundaries on how much and how frequently Lewis tagged him as a second-stringer. The last time, he had almost been blown in half by an Uzi in the Lilac Acres trailer park down by Crowley Street. So he viewed raising the bar as prerequisite to protecting his own ass. For which there was definitely Biblical precedent.

Pearls and swine, after all...

The evidence collection kit was two large plastic tackle boxes full of equipment and containers for collecting and storing crime scene evidence. Barrett and Lewis hauled them out and down the stairs into the basement foundation while the Chief watched. Lewis' first step was to photograph the evidence in situ. Walton returned while this was happening. He spoke briefly to the Chief before joining them down by the discarded bag and shoes.

"No sign of Max. I found his house but it looks like his vehicle recently pulled out. Must be running errands or something."

"I'll follow up this evening by phone," said Lewis. "Meanwhile, let's take a look at what we've got here."

Lewis leaned in close to photograph the running shoes. Then he put the camera aside and pulled rubber gloves from the evidence kit. Leaning in, he grasped a shoe and turned it over, scanning the sole.

"Wear and tear on this baby," he told Walton. "Sabrina walked a lot. And it looks like she walked here."

"Lab should confirm it," said Walton.

"Agreed." Lewis took up both shoes in one hand while holding open a large clear plastic evidence bag with the other. He eased the shoes into the bag then sealed it, noting the date and time on a strip of masking tape across the bag's mouth. Walton walked to the center of the room, turned and examined the stairs.

"You figure she was walked down here? Coerced?" He pointed. "Would have been brought to this locale. Correct?"

"That seems to be the size of it," said Lewis, going on all fours to examine the backpack before disturbing it.

"But you said she walked here." Walton was squinting, focused on whatever didn't add up in his mind.

"You thinking she might have been forced to walk here?" Lewis asked.

"Maybe," said Walton. "Although if you're going to abduct someone, taking them for a nice long walk isn't usually the first step."

Lewis looked up at the Chief. "Who did Sabrina like to hang out with?" he asked.

The Chief thought for a moment. "She was tight with Mary Joe, Jason's sister. I'd see her now and then with the skateboarders, but she never really fit in that group. I think she was also friends with that Mexican girl at high-school, the one whose parents came up on work visas."

"The Andrades family," said Barrett. "They come to Mass sometimes. I can ask around if you like, Gavin."

"I'd appreciate it if you would, padre." Lewis touched the side of the backpack with a gloved forefinger. "Well, lookee there. Strap's broken."

"It wasn't broken when she left for school last time I saw her," said the Chief. "I saw her get on the bus with Mary Joe and the Scanlon twins. She had both straps looped around her shoulders."

The Chief sounded pretty convinced, and Barrett had no reason to doubt the man's memory. However slow and lumbering as he might be on foot, the chief's mental acuity was set at cheetah velocity. The man didn't miss a trick and had a mind like a steel trap.

Lewis went around and squatted by the red sweater. "She was wearing the red sweater that morning, Chief?"

"She was." The Chief nodded. "It was a cool morning. Just before the end of the school year."

"That was the day she went missing." Lewis stood and looked back in the direction of the school. "So we can piece together her final day. She attends school. Comes here—either by her own free will or under duress. We *know* she came down here under duress. Perhaps…" Lewis paused to study the bag and the sweater briefly before turning to the Chief. "I'm going to take a look inside now, Chief. That okay?"

Barrett had to admire the way Lewis did that. He knew tribal members viewed themselves as part of one large, extended family. Involving the Chief in that decision affirmed Lewis' understanding of that and so how much the case meant to the tribe. The Chief nodded and Lewis rooted inside the bag. He began drawing out items, sorting them in neat stacks on the cement floor.

First came the school supplies: three hardback textbooks, a pile of notebooks and a pencil case. (Barrett had to restrain Asshole's curious lunge and sniff.) Next came a folded copy of the high school newspaper. Then came the make-up with the price tags still on them.

"Oh, Sabrina." The Chief sounded sad. "Sergeant Lewis, that stuff would have been shoplifted." ·

"You sound pretty sure." The Mountie was squinting at the Chief. "How do you know?" .

"She was grounded. I remember her mom telling me." The Chief nodded, remembering. "One thing mom had done was take away her make-up. She wasn't allowed to have any. And she's shoplifted before."

"She might have boosted it on the way here," said Barrett. "Which reminds me. When we're done here, I need to talk to you guys about a break-in at the rectory."

"You got robbed?" Lewis sounded surprised. "What did they take?"

"That's the damndest thing! They took toothpaste. Soap. Some of my underwear and socks…"

And to Barrett's surprise, the three other men exploded in laughter.

"What's so goddam funny?" he asked mildly when they were done.

"Sounds like Squatch is back," said Lewis. And this set the three of them to roaring again.

———

"YOU KNOW this town used to be a tourist destination, right?" asked Walton.

Barrett did know. There was a lake nearby with some ruined cottages—a little cluster of summer rentals. The town also had its share of abandoned movie theatres, shops and arcades that once fed off the tourist throng. There was even a rotting midway down near the beach.

"And you know that our tribe, the People of the Otter, have traditions of belief associated with a creature you white men call 'Bigfoot' and 'Sasquatch'?" asked the Chief.

Barrett knew this, too. In fact, Fulton had the distinction of rating high on the world watch-list of Sasquatch sightings. Barrett himself had even been approached by a reporter from a Catholic magazine and asked if he would assent to an interview about the phenomenon from a Catholic perspective. Barrett had declined. Cryptozoology wasn't his kink and besides: there were other, more knowledgeable experts.

"And you know, of course," said Lewis with a twinkle in his eye, "that Fulton wasn't always the bustling economic powerhouse it is today."

"Very funny," sneered Barrett. The town itself was barely clinging to life in the first quarter of the Twenty-First Century. No matter how good the provincial economy was (or wasn't) doing, Fulton remained suspended in a state of near constant semi-recession. Of an average year, six small businesses opened and four closed. The majority of lower middle-class citizens were on welfare. It was not a toddling town, by the stretch of anyone's imagination.

Even that of Sasquatch enthusiasts, Barrett thought.

And they had big imaginations.

"So, the town's decline began not long after Gavin arrived," Walton was saying. His eye held a twinkle, too —a mischievous one. "I'm not saying it's necessarily related, but…"

"Zip it, ass-clown," Lewis shot back, his smirk softening the shot. "It was early in the Bill Clinton era. I remember because there was lots of coverage of his early administration in the news when I got here. Back in the age of television and newspapers."

"All that's changed," said the Chief.

"All that's changed," agreed Walton.

"But Squatch remains," said Lewis. And this time, no one laughed.

The tourist town staggered, then began failing in the early years of the Nineties economic realignment. Fewer and fewer tourists started coming. The shape of the highway was altered, bypassing Fulton. The kitschy summer businesses, which made the bulk of their trade during the sixteen weeks between May Day and Labor Day, began foundering one by one. And it was during this period of economic and cultural transition, in the turmoil of despair and population flight that Lewis came to Fulton and the presence called 'Squatch' began to make itself known.

"I think it was Delmore Leonard who first noted him," said the Chief. "Delmore. He's a fishing fool, is Delmore. Goes every morning. Brings back so much fish. Always shares with the tribe. Always to the widows first, eh? He's a good man. So he said he was coming back through that one property—the cottages down by the lake. First that he passed the shadow of someone in the forest that was running away from the cottages. Then, when he got there, he found one cottage had been broken into. The bathroom. He said the medicine cabinet was pulled open and stuff was scattered around. So this fleeing shadow liked bathrooms and the things inside them. And he moved like a ghost. Like a…"

"Sasquatch," supplied Barrett. "And, let me guess… 'Squatch' for short?"

"You bet."

A pattern of break-ins began. Lewis was fairly sure they were 'talking ninety-four, ninety-five—sometime around there.' "We began tracking break-ins on the updated CPIC database," he offered. "I remember entering one soon after NAFTA came into effect. I read about it in the paper that morning. That was '94. Wintertime. January, February... Around there."

And so it continued, year after year. Usually once in the dead of winter and once again around the summer solstice—someone would break into an empty home and abscond with soap, toilet paper, any spare razors and underwear lying about.

"Kind of an odd choice, don't you think?" asked Barrett.

"Not if you're living rough in the woods," replied Walton. "Which is what we soon figured was going on."

The break-ins continued, concentrated in the cottages near the lake. These dwindled with the decade. By Y2K, there were only two or three per summer. By that time, the tourist colony there was dead and its stash of bathroom and boudoir essentials dwindled to nothing by successive departures and break-ins.

"So Squatch started on our outlying residences," Lewis continued.

The Lilac Acres trailer park was first. Being close-set in by the industrial zone (Avro Lane off of Crowley), they were on the edge of town. So Squatch struck: five trailers in six weeks. Each time: soap, shampoo, underwear.

The week they installed CCTV, he stopped.

"Squatch is a canny sumbitch," Walton concluded. "Knows where to strike, and when. Seems to have an ear to the ground inside the community, although he lives outside it. After all this went down, my files went weird."

"What do you mean, 'went weird'?" Barrett grimaced at Lewis. "That some oh-so-special Conservation Officer talk?"

"Conservation Officers have one of the most

dangerous gigs on the planet," Lewis shot back. "Ninety percent of the people they deal with are armed."

"Fair," allowed Barrett. "But how did things 'go weird'?" he asked Walton.

"We began getting reports of sightings. A lone figure inhabiting the woods. Appearing and then vanishing. A shadow, a rumor. But a persistent presence. Someone was nearby. Living off the grid. Outside of town. Like he was hiding out from something in the forest. We think this was who's responsible for the break-ins." He shrugged. "We started calling him 'Squatch.' As in 'Sasquatch.' Looks like he's back."

Stranger

AT FIRST SUSPICIOUS OF STRANGERS, Asshole eventually became so enamored of Lewis, Walton and the Chief that Barrett had to literally drag him away, claws hissing across concrete, for the return trip home. These feelings seemed mutual. All three men were generous in their praise of the little bulldog, but insufficiently so to adopt him (Barrett tried).

"He's a good boy, father," said the Chief.

"Fine little dog!" affirmed Walton.

"Kinda' looks like you, too, padre," offered Lewis.

Barrett groaned in muted frustration and opted for a detour to the liquor store. Noting the 'NO DOGS' signage, he looped Asshole's leash around a handrail and went in.

"Your dog should be safe there," said the woman behind the counter.

"That's too bad," muttered Barrett, stalking down the row of boxed wines. Selecting a container of his favorite vintage, he walked it up and placed it on the counter by the till.

"That a bulldog?" asked the clerk, ringing up his booze.

"Yes. A miniature, in fact. He's up for adoption, if you're interested…"

"Nah. I have a rabbit." The woman hit the button allowing Barrett to use the keypad for his debit card. "He'd probably kick the shit out of that poor little dog, I tell you what. Man!"

Barrett resumed his trek homeward, Asshole's leash in one hand, the box of wine dangling from the other. If the liquor clerk's rejection hurt the dog, he was giving no sign. Snuffling and farting, he just went on trucking right alongside Barrett.

"Fear not, Asshole," Barrett said quietly. "We'll find you a home."

The dog farted and kept walking, oblivious.

Miss Dolan was, mercifully, gone by the time Barrett returned. He hung Asshole's leash by the door, entered the kitchen and fished his mug from the dish drainer. Then he accessed the spigot of the wine box and sprayed himself a drink. He took a sip and then went for a walk, checking the doors and windows. Miss Dolan had been thorough. The place was dusted and vacuumed, the doors and windows properly secured. A board had even been nailed in place over the broken pane in the laundry room.

Squatch. Barrett rolled the word around in his mind. What a stupid name! But the story itself was interesting. Until recently, Barrett had been very much an urban creature. The ways of rural life had been—and were still —foreign to his experience. That such mysteries could exist, let alone transfix an entire community, was strange to him. But he set aside his immediate bias regarding the poor and uneducated. Walton and Lewis were neither and they seemed on board with the whole 'Squatch' narrative.

It's weird that some guy living in the woods could evade Walton, Barrett thought, wandering through to his study. He took a seat behind the computer, set down his drink and began mousing his way out onto the internet. Reaching a search engine, he typed in his query.

BREAK-INS, FULTON BC

The search engine chewed on the string of words for ten seconds before spitting out a page with the header: [40,000 results].

Whoa, thought Barrett. And began clicking. Most of the links were reprints from or links to stories from the Fulton *Tattler,* the town's twice-weekly newspaper published (and mostly written by) Toby 'Scoop' Jones, Fulton's one and only member of the news media. As a long-standing resident of the town, Scoop had his finger on the pulse of the place. Editions of the *Tattler* Barrett had read contained all the latest about farming and tourism business. But Scoop also had a penchant for reporting on the weird: UFO sightings, livestock mutilations and other unexplained phenomenon. This placed the story in a slightly different light.

But no less compelling for all that, thought Barrett. And began reading.

The first story slightly pre-dated Lewis' but not by long. It was a brief, two paragraph report of a break-in at Shady Acres, the community of holiday cabins that had once done booming business out by the lake a few miles beyond town. One section in particular drew Barrett's notice.

Mr. and Mrs. Gafney, the renters, reported that nothing of real value was taken. "Only some soap and deodorant," said Mrs. Gafney. "And some of my husband's underwear. That's all."

Asshole shambled in, farted and then nosed his way under the desk, where he fell asleep draped over Barrett's foot. Barrett grimaced, took a hard swallow of wine and kept clicking.

Reports picked up and increased the following year. There were more break-ins at Shady Acres. After the fourth, the break-ins rated a feature article. Barrett had a chuckle reading the quote.

"It's extremely unusual for a break-in," said Sergeant Lewis, Fulton's newly-appointed RCMP constable. "When people go to the trouble of doing a break-and-enter, they usually take money or electronics or other valuables. That this individual is taking toiletries suggests perhaps a homeless person. Or maybe a prankster with a weird sense of humor."

The article was accompanied by a photograph of a much younger Lewis. He would have just recently arrived in town. *I bet he was under a lot of pressure,* Barrett thought. Being a newcomer to small towns— particularly a newcomer in an official position—was tricky. Lewis would have found himself besieged by questions, tips, recommendations, admonishments. None of these would help him do his job. But they would serve to make the local citizens feel important as they set about setting this newcomer straight on what was what in their little town.

Barrett kept searching. The articles spooled out over

the years, sometimes as many as six, sometimes as few as two. But the break-ins were a well-known occurrence in Fulton. After a while, they began generating letters to the editor. Somewhere along the line, the name 'Squatch' appeared and was adopted as the moniker for whoever was responsible.

So here's the question, Barrett thought, sitting back and sipping. *If the guy is willing to break into people's homes, what's stopping him from getting into bigger crimes?*

Like abducting youth.

And why not? It made a weird kind of sense. Kidnapping and human trafficking were not common occurrences in the roster of town crime, but that didn't mean they could never happen. What if Squatch suddenly got tired of subsisting on other people's toiletries and decided to splurge? Surely a few missing kids were worth the danger...

Seeing his mug was empty, Barrett rose and navigated his way to the kitchen. Stepping over Asshole slumped in the doorway, he made his way to the counter and was just pouring a refill when the phone rang. Barrett grappled it down from the wall receiver.

"St. Michael and St. Joan's parish. Father Barrett speaking. May I help you?"

"This is Father Michael Barrett?" asked a man's voice on the other end of the line.

"Speaking." Barrett sipped wine and dug for cigarettes.

"Father, we've never met. My name is Anton Stroud. I'm an attorney. I work for Arnold McLellan..."

Oh boy, thought Barrett. *Here we go...*

"...who I believe is currently under your pastoral care at the moment. Is that correct?"

"Yes, I am attending to Mr. McLellan at this time."

Barrett measured his words carefully. As one does when speaking to strange attorneys for the first time.

"Sure. Sure." Stroud sounded conciliatory. "Listen, I'm aware of Mr. McLellan's condition and that he is currently in hospice. He indicated to me that you were his spiritual advisor. And it's for that reason that I'm calling."

"I see. So…" Barrett paused to light a smoke. "What can I do for you?"

"Mr. McLellan has asked me to review a contract with you. It's, ah, a bit unusual. It has to do with his posterity. He's very concerned about his legacy right now."

"That's understandable," Barrett allowed.

"I want to add that the paperwork in question has no direct bearing on you or your parish. But we'd like your view on this. As a…*consultant.* If you like."

"Well, I'm not versed in legal matters, counsellor…"

"Not necessary. It's your expertise as a pastor that we're interested in. Probably take no more than fifteen minutes. Are you home now?"

"Well, yes. I—"

"I'll be there in fifteen minutes," Stroud said. And hung up.

Barrett yanked the receiver away from his ear as the dial tone blared, glaring at the phone in disgust. *I'll be there in fifteen minutes?* What kind of attorney says something like that?

The kind who's getting paid big bucks, Barrett thought.

He wandered back to his study and resumed his research on Squatch.

The figure certainly generated his share of controversy. Barrett found a mother lode of letters to the editor dating back a decade or so. Based on tone,

Squatch was not generating a great deal of local goodwill.

> ...*am disgusted at the lack of concern shown by local authorities at the blatant lawlessness exhibited by this thief!*

> ...*probably homeless. We wouldn't be in this position if the province did more to address the challenges facing the unhoused...*

> ...*pay good money for rent and food! Part of that is taxes! When are the police going to wake up and do something about...*

The more recent the letters, the less they had to do with the break-ins themselves. The crimes became an anchor of resentment from which tangents launched. The longer the Squatch figure remained at large, the more he became symbolic of everyone's pet peeves. As the decades rolled on, he was blamed for everything from forest fires to the poor showing of students in standardized provincial testing. Squatch sure got around. *Talk about a productive career in mischief,* Barrett thought.

And then, abruptly, the letters stopped. As did any news coverage of the break-ins.

They must have stopped, Barrett stopped. *Either that or they simply were no longer of interest.*

Weird!

There was nothing about the rectory break-in. There was at least that.

I've got to get some more info on those sightings Walton talked about, Barrett thought. The Conservation Officer had mentioned rumors of somebody living in the woods outside of Fulton. That wasn't entirely uncommon. Campers came and went. The local homeless occasionally ventured out that way with dreams of setting up a utopia in the trees. And there were hippies that showed up and colonized the various garden spots for their naked, pot-fuelled frolics among the fauna. Somehow, Squatch stood out from all that. Barrett decided to do what he could to understand why that was.

Asshole began barking at the top of his lungs.

Barrett sighed, downed the last of his wine and shuffled into the kitchen. There was, as usual, a full pot of coffee bubbling on the percolator. Barrett poured himself a cup and wandered into the front room to see what the din was all about.

Asshole was perched on his ample ass, the toes of his front paws spread like he was gripping the floor as he barked repeatedly. Each yip strained the little mutt. Barrett knelt down and soothed the beast with a pat on the head.

"Relax there, buddy." Barrett fought down a surge of fondness for the little bulldog. "We're in no danger…"

He heard a car door slam and rose to his feet.

A navy-blue Cadillac was parked at the curb outside. Barrett watched as the driver produced a fob from his pocket and armed the car with the push of a button. Barrett studied the figure as he approached. The man was slender, bald, and adorned in the most expensive suit Barrett had seen in some time. He wore a pair of mirrored shades. The watch on his wrist and the briefcase that dangled from one arm was probably worth more than the parish Hyundai. Barrett waited with interest to see what he wanted.

Stroud

BARRETT OPENED the door and watched him approach.

"Father Barrett?" The man looked up and plucked off the sunglasses, flashing a dazzling smile that reeked of charm and bullshit. "Anton Stroud, attorney-at-law." He extended a hand.

"Michael Barrett." As an afterthought, he added: "SJ." It seemed an appropriate response to 'Attorney-at-Law.' *Since we're flashing credentials.* He shook. "Please come in. Can I offer you a cup of coffee?"

Stroud, pocketing his sunglasses, appeared inclined to refuse then reconsidered. "Sure. A cup of coffee sounds delightful."

"How do you take yours, counsellor?"

"I ordinarily only drink espresso. But black will do fine."

"Black. As in…and white. Appropriate for the legal profession."

"Or religion." Stroud peered down his nose. "Both are disciplines which deal in absolutes."

"I'd disagree, counsellor." Barrett smiled. "You deal in temporal reality. *I* deal in absolutes."

Stroud seemed on the point of arguing, but he acceded the point with a gracious wave of the hand. Barrett fetched him a mug and refreshed his own, pouring coffee over the lees of his wine. When Barrett returned to the front room, he saw that Stroud had helped himself to a seat on the couch and placed his briefcase on the coffee table.

"Ah, thank you!" Stroud accepted the mug and took a surreptitious sniff. "Is this fair trade coffee?"

"It's coffee my housekeeper buys."

"Really?" Stroud sounded impressed. "So you get a housekeeper? In addition to this house?"

"It's a package deal. Like the church. It comes along with a deacon and a lector. And a substantial helping of legacy politics."

"It's been said that religion and politics are two sides of the same coin!" Whether it was fair trade or not, Stroud sipped his coffee anyway.

"Coins aren't much in use these days," countered Barrett. "You could say two sides of the same bill, but even that's being replaced."

"Mm. You mean crypto currency. Tell me, father. Do churches still pass the donation basket on Sunday?"

"Sure." Barrett smiled. "Although some of my younger parishioners prefer to do a bank transfer or use PayPal."

"Imagine that," Stroud said flatly. "The church fails to adapt socially and politically. But when it comes to money…"

Barrett imagined the observation was intended to rile him, but it was one he'd made himself many times. So, he just toasted Stroud and sipped Merlot-flavored coffee.

"So how have your sessions with Mr. McLellan been going?" Stroud asked.

"Good. I would say. Ministering to people at the end of their lives is never easy. But Mr. McLellan is eager to receive pastoral care. And I'm helping out where I can, here and there."

"But you wouldn't characterize Arnold as a death bed convert, now. Would you?" Stroud's teasing smile appeared above the rim of his cup.

"I wouldn't even characterize Mr. McLellan as a Christian."

"No. I don't suppose so." Stroud foraged in his brief-case and drew out a file folder. "And, really, why should he be? No offense, father. But religion is a replacement for worldly success. People who are busy being productive and successful don't have time to get on their knees and chatter at God."

"I would suggest that productive and successful people should be doing just that. Out of gratitude."

"Gratitude?" Stroud's expression hovered on the edge of shock before dissolving into laughter. "Isn't it the other way around? Shouldn't the gratitude be flowing Mr. McLellan's way? After all he's done for this town? For your church?"

"We are grateful for Mr. McLellan's bequests." Barrett reflected on the check for one thousand dollars that appeared shortly after he began his pastoral visits. "And no doubt the citizens of Fulton are grateful to him, as well. For jobs. For opportunities. He is, as you say, 'a big fish.' But Fulton is a small pond. So," Barrett concluded, "is the Earth."

"Ah! The Jesuitical mind." Stroud's tone held real approval. "I had a Jesuit professor as an undergraduate. Enormously clever man. He spent half the semester proving the existence of God. And the other half disproving it. It was edifying."

"How so?"

"It exposed me to the elasticity of the religious mind." Stroud opened the folder and began sorting papers. "You must admit, father. The church has been flexible throughout history. You're real survivors. How long have you bunch been in business? Two thousand years or so?"

"Oldest corporation on Earth," Barrett said, toasting him. As an afterthought, he added: "Over two billion saved."

"And how does one remain in business that long? I would suggest it's by recognizing the political and legal realities of the moment and adapting." Barrett could tell from Stroud's tone and posture that he was ready to get down to business. "The church has a history of mediating between Man and God. Sometimes these arrangements have been financial in nature, correct?"

"You're talking about indulgences?" Barrett frowned. "Listen, counsellor. We got out of that business a long, *long* time ago. It was an error in our policies that was later corrected."

"But the communication lines are still open? I mean, priests *do* intercede for people."

"What are you getting at, Mr. Stroud?"

The attorney allowed himself a sour little smile as he closed his briefcase and set the folder down on top of it.

"Father, you know Mr. McLellan's—*Arnold's*—situation as well as I do. Perhaps even better, in some ways. The man is dying. He hasn't much time left. And he's been reading that copy of the Bible you provided for him…"

"Glad to hear it!"

"Yes…I think it's fair to say he understands what's at stake. And he's in fear for what lies next."

Barrett drew in a sharp breath. This was the first indication he had received from anyone that McLellan was beginning to loose his hold on worldly matters to focus on the eternal. That fear was involved troubled Barrett. He despised the use of fear to coerce people into 'believing.' That just sat wrongly with him. But in this case, the fear seemed entirely self-made on McLellan's part.

"Death." Stroud opened the folder. "Final judgment. There *is* a judgment involved, isn't there?"

"Yes, counsellor."

"So." Stroud smiled. "Now we're in *my* territory. Trial and judgment are my bread and butter. And as Mr. McLellan has been my client for over a decade, I am doing everything I can to place him in a strong position going into court."

"Well, that's *my* territory, actually…"

"And what comfort have you given him?" Stroud sniffed. "Arnold is petrified of eternal damnation. He can't get his mind around believing in God. And without that, he goes to Hell. Isn't that the way it works?"

"'*No man comes to the Father except by me,*'" Barrett quoted. "Christianity posits a belief in Christ is necessary to endure the rigors of the afterlife."

"And if a man can't?"

"That's in God's hands." Barrett shrugged gently. "I don't claim to know God's ways. Only what I've been told. What I've *read.*"

"I've read it, too." Stroud studied the papers in the folder before him. "And I believe I've found a loophole."

"A 'loophole'?" Barrett laughed. "It doesn't work…"

"Of course it does! Every legal system has its codicils, its addendums and clauses, its escape hatches. My client wants to avoid Hell."

Barrett waited, unable to fathom where Stroud was going with this.

"He has asked me to draw up a contract." Stroud picked up one set of papers and handed it across. "I've brought a copy here for your review."

Barrett blinked. Had he just heard correctly? Stroud was proposing some kind of binding agreement between himself and the Almighty in exchange for passage into Heaven? He took the documents and examined the top sheet, frowning.

This agreement, undertaken between ARNOLD MCLELLAN (hereafter, the Party of the First Part) and THE LORD GOD ALMIGHTY (hereafter, the Party of the Second Part) is to formalize and ensure the post-mortem passage from Earth and acceptance into Heaven of the Party of the First Part by the Party of the Second Part…

Barrett looked up. "You can't be serious."

Stroud said nothing.

Barrett laughed. "Arnold McLellan wants to negotiate a *contract*? With *God?*"

"Well, why not?" Stroud spread his hands. "The Bible is full of contracts. Just by another name. They're called covenants, aren't they? Think of the agreements between God and Abraham, between God and Moses…"

"That's different."

"How?" Stroud had the bit between his teeth now. "Abraham was a man. So was Moses."

"They were prophets."

"So? Prophets are men."

"Arnold McLellan…" Barrett set down the agreement. "Is no prophet."

"But he's *made* profits."

Barrett groaned at Stroud's sophomoric wordplay.

"For himself. For his family. For his community. And, I might add, for your church."

"So you want…*what* from me? Exactly."

"We want you to review and sign the contract on behalf of the Party of the Second Part."

Barrett guffawed. It was the most ridiculous request ever made of him by a parishioner. Or anyone else, for that matter.

Stroud was studying him as his laughing jag ended. "What's so funny?" he asked.

"This!" Barrett thumped the pages before him on the coffee table. "First of all, the idea that we're in a position to bargain with God is ridiculous. That's not how God works. One *accepts* God's terms and then *receives* His Grace. One does not extort acceptance from God."

"This is in exchange for a $25,000 bequest to the church." Stroud smiled. "No extortion involved."

"McLellan wants to buy an indulgence." Barrett shook his head firmly. "No. Sorry, counsellor. But the church stopped doing that 500 years ago. We're, ah, no longer in that line of work, so to speak…"

"Fine." Stroud gathered up the papers. "Then who should I speak to?"

Barrett considered. McLellan's move was a ridiculous one—a move born of desperation and fear. The last move of a wealthy man discovering, on death's door, that you can't take it with you. It was almost…

Sad. Barrett sniffed. *But a $25,000 bequest…*

"Okay, look." Barrett held up his hands. "I could refer you to my superiors, but chances are your correspondence will just end up in the inbox, collecting dust. Allow me…" He reached. "To present it to Archbishop Crowe. He's Archbishop of the Grand Diocese of Vancouver and my superior. I'll discuss the offer with him and have him get back to you. Fair?"

Stroud hesitated, then picked up a copy of the contract and handed it over. "Alright, Father Barrett." Stroud slipped the rest into his briefcase and latched it up. "That's acceptable to my client. We'll wait to hear from Archbishop…Crowe, you said?"

"Yes. Crowe. Andrew Crowe." Barrett sighed. "I'll scan this and send it to him via e-mail this afternoon."

"Fine." Stroud stood and shook hands, then left.

Barrett sighed, took up the contract and both coffee cups and went into the kitchen. He poured the remainder of his coffee down the sink and poured himself a fresh mug of wine. Then he went downstairs to his office.

It only took him a few minutes to scan the contract and compose an e-mail to the Archbishop. He copied Brother Steven, Crowe's assistant, then laid in a call to him.

"Archbishop's office."

"Brother Steven? It's Michael Barrett in Fulton. Just wanted to send you a head's up. There's an e-mail coming your way that has to do with a bequest to the church. I'd appreciate it if the Archbishop could read and respond to it as quickly as possible."

"Of course," replied Brother Steven smoothly. "That's something I'm sure the Archbishop will take an immediate interest in. I'll make sure he sees it post haste."

"Great. Thanks."

Barrett hung up and drained his wine. Then he went upstairs and poured himself another. Deciding himself to be in need of rest, he settled before the TV. He was halfway through his next cup of wine when he passed out.

Cauchemar

BARRETT WAS DREAMING.

Not something he did often. Whenever he did lay him down to sleep, the booze tended to keep him drifting in and out of the slipstream just above REM. Barrett's sleeping habits were inconsistent and transitory, at best. He was plagued by persistent fatigue. So when his mind finally rebelled sufficiently to plunge him into the depth of dreams, it usually did so with force and brutal finality.

Tonight was no different.

———

HE WALKED A VAST STONE CORRIDOR. *Barrett couldn't tell what sort of stone, but it was intimidating. Dark, rough-hewn, it had the sinister, forbidding feel of boulders hauled from the guts of a volcano—something about it spoke of fire and chains and fitful misery. They rose into shadowed distance, their tops lost in vapor and dark. The ground underfoot was hewn of the same stone but cut with a garish red carpet with gold trim—the sort of thing celebrities paraded across at one of their never-ending festivals of self-congratulation. (The Oscars? The Emmys? The Tonys? The Pansies? Barrett couldn't recall…)*

Lining either side of the corridor were a series of doors. Oaken and heavy, they reminded him of church doors. They were about that heavy. But rectangular and furnished with the usual knob arrangement, they were more suited to executive offices or perhaps upscale hotel rooms. He noted that the doors were unmarked…

But, wait. No, they weren't. The doors did have identifying symbols on them, but they were strange, meaningless glyphs. Barrett paused and examined one. It was obsidian black against the dark oak tone of the door and made of some strange oil-like substance. Barrett squinted, trying to read the symbol. But as he did, it shifted, changing shape into something else Barrett couldn't read, either. It was the same story with the next door. And the next. So Barrett resumed walking down the forbidding stone corridor.

The sound of children whispering together rose. There was something sinister in the sound. Barrett, who had never cared for children, had nonetheless grown accustomed to them and their chaotic ways during his post-seminary stint teaching in a large public high school. But something about these whispers were different. They had a stygian quality, like a coven of witches conferring in secret amongst themselves.

Barrett stopped to listen. And the voices stopped, too.

Then one of the doors opened. It just…fell back on its hinges, swinging wide. Smoke or fog swirled just beyond the jamb. Barrett squinted into the miasma until he could make out the figure of a person just inside. A small and slender person…

A girl.

And she was suffering.

Pain etched her features, lending them an ancient look although the girl could not have been more than ten. She stood in a pyjama onesie, a teddy-bear gripped under one arm, a look of anguish on her face. When she opened her mouth, Barrett knew it was to scream. Jesus, the poor kid! What was wrong? Barrett moved to help...

And the door closed.

Barrett lunged for the door and raised his fist to knock. But before he could, some strange power compelled him to turn and keep walking. Against his will, he proceeded. The carpet rolled past below his feet. He turned his head to one side in time to see another door open. Again, there was a child there...

Weeping. Bleeding. Raising his hands and imploring Barrett for help. Barrett gasped, turning toward the child, hands reaching out to take him in his arms and render aid. He lowered himself pre-emptively to accommodate the difference in height and the door...

Closed again. The one beside it opened.

Another child, this one also in anguish. Barrett moved to help and was met by another closing door. He felt tears crowding the backs of his eyes. The next child was obviously a victim of war; Barrett could see the injuries just before the door...

Closed.

His breathing quickened. A darkness was descending over the corridor. Suddenly, the carpet below him was broken by a set of stairs that appeared magically at his feet. Barrett squared his shoulders and descended as the doors behind him opened, loosing the sound of children wailing in anguish. Barrett attempted to turn back but was impelled by the same force that pushed him down the corridor to descend into darkness.

He clambered down. It seemed to take forever. Much of the journey occurred in pitch blackness, but this was eventually broken by a light. The closer Barrett came to it, the more he recognized the glow for what it was.

Candlelight, he realized.

The steps terminated in a vast, low-ceilinged room ringed by elaborate iron candelabra. Red and black candles flickered, throwing a weird glow upon the triangular table at the center of the room. Drawn up in chairs before the table was a group of robed and cowled men. He knew at once these men were evil.

A chill gripped Barrett's heart.

He sensed the dream ending. The scene was fading. But not before he witnessed a parchment scroll unrolled and placed before one of the men, who took up a quill and dipped it into a bottle of red (blood) ink. He slowly and laboriously signed his name. It appeared in the same weird glyph pattern Barrett had seen on the doors in the corridor upstairs. Protean, shifting, it crawled across the page, changing shape even as the scroll was rolled up. Just as Barrett navigated the last distance between the scene and wakefulness, he watched the robed man rise and take possession of a chain that somebody handed to him—a chain looped to an iron ring. An iron ring around the neck of a child…

Horror enflamed Barrett. He reached out a hand but consciousness swirled around him until he…

———

…CAME AWAKE WITH A SHUDDERING GROAN.

Christ!

The last scene from the dream still eddied in his mind, chilling his heart. Cold with horrors, he looked around. He was still in front of the television, his half-empty mug of wine beside him. The movie he had been watching had been replaced by a weather report. Barrett squinted at the time in the lower right-hand corner of the screen beside the word-crawl.

Jesus, five-thirty AM? he thought. *Did I sleep through the entire night?*

The sound of a car crawling up the driveway made him catch his breath. *Miss Dolan!* At this hour of the morning, she usually arrived in time to make him breakfast. He couldn't let her see him like this! Rising unsteadily, he snatched up his mug and hurried into the kitchen. Stepping to the sink, he made as if to pour the rest of his wine down the drain before hesitating, upending the cup and swallowing it down. Then he rinsed the mug, set it in the dish drainer, lifted the wine box back into the cupboard above the sink and fled into the washroom just in time to avoid her entrance.

Barrett locked the door behind him and sank down on the closed lid of the john. He was still trembling from the combined shock of the nightmare, the sudden movements upon awakening and the punch of the wine hitting his system.

That was a close-run thing, he thought.

He heard the rattle of the trash can as Miss Doyle opened it and removed the bag. Barrett waited until she had exited through the wide door to place it in the outdoor bin to emerge. Moving quickly, he put on his jacket, grabbed Asshole's leash and clipped it to the bulldog's collar where he lay in the kitchen doorway. He managed to let himself out the front door, dragging Asshole behind him, just as Miss Doyle was returning inside.

Coffee, Barrett thought. *I need coffee. I'll head down to the donut shop.*

"Come on, Asshole," he said, tugging the leash. "Let's go get some grub."

Asshole shook himself, looked up at Barrett, and licked his lips.

"If you're good, I'll get you a donut."

As if understanding, the bulldog was on his best behavior as Barrett walked down the block and turned the corner onto Fulton's main drag. Most of the stores and restaurants were closed at this hour. But the neon rectangle of McBride's Donut Shoppe was lit and the sign in the door turned to OPEN. Barrett let himself in. He was the only customer in the place.

"G'morning, father." Gene McBride looked up from the cash register, then dubiously down at Asshole. "We, ah, normally don't let dogs in here…"

"Oh. Sorry. Can I, uh, get something to go, then?"

"Sure, father." McBride smiled. "Guess I can make an exception just this once. What'll you have?"

"Large black coffee and one of those cream-filled Boston things."

Asshole whined and twisted at his leash.

"Oh." Barrett glanced down. "And a, uh, powdered donut for my dog."

"Your dog eats donuts?"

"My dog eats anything."

McBride shrugged and set him up with his order. Barrett paid, took up his coffee and bag of donuts, then led Asshole out the door and down the street to a bench he knew. Shadowed by the taller buildings in this area of town, the bench inhabited a bower of darkness where night lingered. Barrett sat, placed his bag of donuts beside him and took a sip of coffee. The nightmare had faded completely now, save for the emotional residue, and Barrett was just that much closer to having his head back on straight.

The subconscious mind is a tricky thing, he thought. He struggled to remember details of the dream and caught only flashes: doors, children, robed men signing documents...

Weird!

A low rumbling intruded. Barrett looked up the street in time to see a motorcycle approach. He recognized the distinctive sound of a Harley Davidson. The bike slowed as soon as its headlamp caught him.

"Hey, father!" The biker pulled up to the curb and shut off the engine. Barrett squinted at the figure silhouetted behind the light. The voice was familiar. That's when he placed the man.

"Mick!" Barrett smiled and rose, coffee cup in hand. Big Mick Hudson was the president of the Paladins, a biker gang headquartered in the forests outside of Fulton. Those boys normally partied into the wee hours. What Mick was doing out at this time of morning was anyone's guess.

"Boy, am I glad I bumped into you." Mick switched off the light and dismounted. Barrett could see the biker was shaken.

"What's the matter?" Barrett had had more contact with Mick and his outlaw gang than was probably wise for a priest. Their paths had crossed last fall, when Barrett helped the man locate his missing daughter.

"I just got back from Nanaimo, man." Mick shook his head. "Just up visiting some brothers, ya' know? Checking on some business. I heard something *really* sick, padre."

"Oh?" Barrett held up the bag. "Care for a donut?"

"Nah. I'm good." Mick drew a joint out from behind his ear and lit it, perfuming the pre-dawn street in clouds of cannabis. "Thing of it is, father... The Vietnamese gangs are back, working the dock front."

"I thought the Red and Whites drove them all out," Barrett said. He had read about the Hell's Angels' confrontation with Vietnamese criminal gangs in the newspaper.

"I thought so, too. But they're back." Mick sucked on his doobie. "They got a new game going. They're done muscling in on our territory. Now they're into something worse."

"What?"

"Human trafficking, man." Mick's jaw firmed as he spoke. "Word is they're snatching kids and selling them on the black market. The sick fucks! What kind of person would *do* something like that, man?"

"Funny you should mention that," Barrett said casually. "I've been wondering the same thing myself, lately."

He took out his Boston cream and ate a thoughtful bite.

Baphomet

"STILL GOT THAT DOG?" Gavin Lewis smirked as he stirred his coffee, watching Barrett enter the detachment office with Asshole trailing behind him, snuffling and farting. Walton, seated at his desk, stifled a snort and sipped his own cup.

"Yeah." Barrett closed the door behind him and gazed down at the bulldog. "You guys like to hunt, right? I've never been hunting. But I understand that dogs are often used to—"

Lewis nearly spat out his coffee laughing.

"—to...to track game. And chase away predators... Perhaps, you know, this dog could be trained to do...that?"

Walton threw back his head and guffawed. "'Chase away predators'? Padre, have you actually been in the woods around here?"

Lewis, meanwhile, was laughing so hard he had to grab the desk to stay upright. Asshole, oblivious to all this, dropped down on his rump, raised a leg and began licking his balls.

"Oh, I dunno, Adam," offered Lewis between chuckles. "He could keep rabbits away from the camp."

"Sure! And squirrels." Walton was trying hard to keep a straight face. "He'd be useful to us, sure. Until he fell down a hole."

"Or a moose stepped on him."

Barrett endured their uproarious hilarity patiently, reminding himself of St. Sebastian and Joan of Arc. *Burned at the stake,* he thought. *For the simple crime of trying to rid myself of...*

He looked down. Asshole looked up at him, licked his lips, and farted.

God, this dog is a walking disaster area.

"Okay." He held up his hands. "You've had your fun. It was just an idea. Now how about a cup of coffee for your patient, long-suffering local priest? I have some things to discuss with you related to those missing Native kids."

"Help yourself, padre," said Lewis, gesturing toward the coffee station with his cup. Then he bent and rooted in his desk. "Come to think of it, I have a bag of dog treats in here somewhere..." He pulled out a zip-lock bag of milk-bones. "Here we are. *Here,* pup. Come on..."

Gavin extended a milk-bone toward Asshole. The little bulldog immediately spun and bared his fangs, growling.

"Okay, then. Fuck you." Lewis dropped the bag back into the drawer and banged it shut. "Must say, father. That dog sure is loyal to you..."

"At least I have that going for me," Barrett muttered. He filled a coffee cup and took a seat by Lewis' desk. "So, both of the missing youngsters are First Nations."

"Yeah." Lewis pulled a folder across the desk and

opened it. "Jason Joe and Sabrina. Both in the past month and both members of the local tribe. It doesn't fit the pattern of missing and murdered First Nations across the rest of the province."

"Why's that?" Barrett sipped his coffee and broke off a bit of powdered donut for Asshole to eat.

"The majority of those cases are on the mainland." Lewis shrugged. "A great many are clustered around the so-called 'Highway of Tears.' Of course, First Nations go missing here on the island, too. But those are mostly tribes that live closer to population centers like Victoria or Duncan. The People of the Otter are isolated, even by Native standards. They've been spared a lot of that."

"They don't tend to go missing?"

"Nah." Lewis made a dismissive wave of the hand. "They're a close-knit bunch. The Chief is laid back but has eyes like a hawk. Last missing persons case we had from them was two years back." He glanced at Walton. "Remember Adrian Robert?"

"Sure do." Walton swivelled in his chair to examine the regional map pinned to the bulletin board behind his desk. "He wasn't gone long, as I recall. Only a few days. They found him out by the lake."

"The tribe found him by themselves," said Lewis. "Those people know this area and each other very well. They take care of their own. That they found him that quick was damned impressive, even by police standards. So for two kids to go missing…"

"I've had word from a reliable source that Vietnamese criminal gangs are operating again in Nanaimo."

Lewis and Walton shared a glance.

"How did you know that, padre?" Lewis was genuinely surprised. "Only RCMP and local by-law enforcement have been briefed on that."

"I have a CI."

"Who?"

Barrett smiled and shook his head as he held up a hand.

"Alright. Fair enough," said Lewis. Keeping confidential informants anonymous was a common courtesy among investigators. "I'm guessing, given the CIs you used on your last case that your current one is a little on the shady side."

"Small-time member of the criminal element." Barrett blew on his coffee. "Says the Viets are kidnapping and trafficking people."

Lewis sat very still. Walton was watching him carefully. Barrett started to feel a little uncomfortable.

"Your CI is good," Lewis said at length. "RCMP sent two detectives from the mainland. E-Division, major crimes section. They're heading up a human trafficking task force in the Nanaimo detachment. That's B-level clearance, padre. Nobody's supposed to know that."

"Have you been in touch with them on this case?"

"No." Lewis' tone held a note of caution.

"Okay." Barrett, knowing how clannish Mounties tended to be, let that one lie. "Seems to me we could have two cases that are possibly related. But that's in your hands, Gavin..."

"I'll talk to them," Lewis replied quickly. "If we got kids going missing, I'm covering every angle. We'll get their names on the task force watch-list. It can't do any harm."

Walton stood and went to the map. "I've been keeping an eye open on my conservation patrols," he said. He jabbed a finger at a sector of the woods south of town. "I've been concentrating here. But I'm thinking perhaps I should go back towards the lake. Those ruined cabins at the old Shady Acres vacation community—the ones Squatch used to break into—would make a great staging area for human traffickers fishing for prey around here. I'll check it out."

Both lawmen turned to Barrett.

"I think I'm going to go back and poke around that housing development. What's it called again? Spirit Ranch Estates? I'll bring along my trusty assistant, here…"

Lewis was chuckling again. "Don't think he's much suited for work as a police dog, padre…"

"He's not suited for much at all," Barrett sighed. "Aside from annoying people."

———

WHEN BARRETT EMERGED from the joint RCMP/Conservation detachment office, the sun had risen and the town was coming to life. He grappled a pair of Ray-Bans from his jacket pocket and shoved them into place over his eyes. Then he and the dog struck off down the sidewalk in the direction of Spirit Ranch Estates.

Main Street was a jumble of offices and boutique shops. Barrett wandered past the open copy shop and the marijuana dispensary. The Service Canada building remained closed, a line of welfare recipients already forming outside the front door. At the intersection beyond, McLellan's beckoned. The faux big-box store, another of Arnold McLellan's investments and the main retail outlet in Fulton, was already doing brisk business, shoppers going in and out, some with carts laden. He kept walking. The liquor store was not yet open. Barrett checked his watch. He would have to come back later.

He went down two blocks, turned a corner and found the long, curving road that led up the hill to the housing development.

The weird, preternatural stillness of the place hit him even before it came into sight. *Spirit Ranch.* Barrett disliked the name. It reeked of yuppie woo-woo, New Age-y bullshit. *Why are the laptop class so obsessed with every spiritual path in the world but the one they were born into?* Barrett wondered. He figured it probably had something to do with the costumes and props. In traditional Christianity, such things were reserved for the priesthood. In New Age and pagan rites, they were available to the average worshipper.

Breaking down the wall between priest and worshipper is how it starts, Barrett guessed. *From there it's an easy trek to breaking down walls between faiths. My Buddhism is just as good as your Catholicism...my paganism...my Satan worship...*

Barrett had never been one for ecumenism. Especially when it led to bestowing dumb-shit names on housing developments—ones likely to be inhabited by white collar professionals. Barrett, who avoided people in general, reserved a special dislike for executives, bureaucrats and tech types. He found them condescendingly shallow and out of touch. A species of such people even existed within the hierarchy of the church.

Barrett avoided them, too.

Now he was back in the land of cute model homes and faux-ranch fencing. A chorus of lawn sprinklers hissed to life like a clutch of snakes as Barrett passed, prompting a barking jag from Asshole. Barrett sighed and kept walking. The damn dog was useless!

He passed the row of completed houses and angled toward the half-built units in which the backpack and shoes had been found. The site had been quickly abandoned and left in disarray following the legal collision of McLellan and the tribe. Foundations and half-completed basements covered the grounds and stark wooden frames groped the sky. Barrett paused at the one basement he'd visited with Lewis. It was ringed with yellow police tape. Glancing inside, Barrett saw nothing new so pressed on.

It was the sort of area, he reflected, that would be attractive to kids. There were places to clamber around and explore, windows to break, surfaces just begging for graffiti. Barrett saw traces of such shenanigans, but nothing major. Or recent. He kept walking.

A larger partially-completed foundation loomed ahead—a vast rectangle in the ground, this one obviously intended as the basement of an up-scale unit. *They probably have different models in mind,* he thought. *Two-bedroom versus three-bedroom and so forth.* This one must be for a deluxe model: the basement included a few completed cinderblock rooms. Barrett decided to pause and do a little exploring.

A set of concrete steps had been finished. It was a long way down and missing handrails, but Barrett negotiated them carefully, pulling the dog along behind him. They descended to the floor and looked around.

This basement was big enough to be a house unto itself. Barrett noted the plumbing access pipes and the reinforced surfaces meant to hold water tanks, oil heaters and the like. Beyond lay two of the cinderblock rooms. As Barrett approached the first one, Asshole abruptly began barking.

"Oh, for God sake…" Barrett stopped and turned. "What…"

Then he realized: the dog was barking at the door of the nearest room.

Is it possible he actually senses something?

Barrett edged toward the door. The room had a rough ceiling installed, blocking out the light. But even in the dimness, a shape was visible on the floor inside.

Barrett grappled his lighter from his pocket and flicked it on. It punched a globe of light into the dark. Barrett squinted at the shape on the floor. *Too small to be a body,* he thought. This was confirmed as he approached. It wasn't a person but a piece of clothing. *It's a hoodie!*

Barrett knelt. Reaching out, he felt the rough texture of the stout hoodie's material. It was red. He grasped and tugged, the hoodie unfurling as it rolled toward him. On the front was a stylized feather and the words: NATIVE PRIDE.

Kid size, he realized. That's when his eye caught sight of a shape on the wall.

Barrett examined it in the glow from his lighter. Someone had painted something on the cinderblocks. He held up his lighter…then held his breath. He recognized the inverted, five-pointed star known as a 'Baphomet.' Symbolic of the Sabbatic goat, it was a glyph commonly associated with Satanic worship.

A footstep scuffed the floor behind him. Barrett half-turned before the blow descended that knocked him unconscious.

"Other People's Secrets..."

BARRETT WRESTLED his way to consciousness, aware of a splitting headache and a pinching at his right wrist. *Asshole?* He figured it must be the dog's leash, because that was the last thing he remembered having looped around the wrist. But when he tugged, instead of the flexible give of the leash leather, he felt a sharp flash of pain shoot up his right arm. He groaned, only half-awake. As the pain numbed, he grew aware of other sensations in his body: the tightness of his legs, the cramp in his torso, the ache from the blow that had laid him out. He found his face muscles, flexed his cheeks and opened his eyes.

He appeared to be lying on a couch—one of those Victorian leather numbers with the elaborate wooden scrollwork along its arms and back. The wrist pain came from the handcuffs.

Barrett swung around from a lying to a seated position and examined the restraints. They were not the standard issue, dull battleship gray cuffs police used. These were black titanium, new and shiny.

Whoever's kidnapped me has exquisite taste in furniture and handcuffs, he thought.

He looked around.

The room was large—two stories high and split-level, ringed by a balcony enclosed by an elaborate banister. Tall bookshelves lined the walls. There were more shelves on the level above, which was connected to the floor below by a spiral staircase. A wheeled ladder was visible by the nearest shelf. The combination of fine oak populated by exquisite leather-bound volumes produced a distinct atmospheric ambiance. Barrett doubted he had ever seen a more handsome personal library.

The guy who lives here must be flush, Barrett thought. *This is in a mansion somewhere.*

He longed for a cigarette. But the logistics of producing a pack and lighting it one-handed proved too daunting to contemplate just now. So he returned to his original problem...

Where the hell *was* he?

A smarting pain flared at the back of his skull. He raised his left hand and probed softly with fingertips and drew them back, smeared and sticky. *Blood.* He knew it by texture and scent. A small gash had opened in the flesh above and behind his right ear. He remembered the blow—the hard finality of impact. He had been struck with some hard, blunt object. He checked for concussion by drawing a few hard breaths and half-standing. Encountering no dizziness, he felt relief. The blow had been clean and professionally delivered. Which suggested a whole new set of problems.

I've been snatched. The question is...

A door opened at the far end of the room.

By whom?

Barrett braced himself. A figure entered, indistinct in

the shadows, followed by another and another. The line of men entered, each wearing hooded robes. And his heart *(robed men seated at a table)* clutched in memory of the dream…*(signing a document in blood)*…and froze his breath.

The robed figures approached, all identical in their sinister silence. They arrayed themselves around the couch in a semi-circle. Barrett counted thirteen. He flashed on the inverted pentagram adorning the basement wall, the child's hoodie and the significance of the number. He had never been a superstitious man. But…

Thirteen. Traditional number for a witches' coven, he recalled from seminary class on cults and Satanism. *And now they have a Catholic priest at their mercy…*

Barrett's jaw firmed.

He was no ordinary Catholic priest.

These bastards were in for a surprise.

Movement. One of the men withdrew a long, thick candle from his robe and lit it. In its glow, Barrett could see another man draw a curved knife from beneath his robe. Its blade glimmered in the candlelight. A third man stepped forward from the group and approached Barrett.

"You are Father Michael Barrett of the parish of St. Michael and St. Joan," intoned a voice from within the shadows of the hood.

"I'm sorry," replied Barrett. "But I don't speak to people who refuse to show their faces during a conversation."

"You don't have to speak," said the man. "In fact, it would be better if you didn't. You weren't brought here to talk. You were brought here to listen."

"Oh, yeah? Is that the reason for all the cloak and dagger bullshit?" He jerked his chin at the man with the knife. "And I mean that literally. Christ! Can Freddy Kruger over there put his goddam knife away? I feel like I'm in a low budget horror film."

The hooded man did not reply. He let the statement end. And the ensuing silence fill with deeper silence.

Barrett waited.

"You're a very curious priest. Aren't you." It wasn't a question. The hooded man folded his hands. "Always out and about. With that dog of yours. Exploring the town and sticking your nose in where it doesn't belong and where it's not wanted."

"What can I say? I'm just a curious guy." Despite his predicament, Barrett was beginning to tire of the men's theatrics.

"You know that old saying about curiosity. And cats."

"Is that a threat?"

"Your explorations," the man continued, "have led you where you are not wanted. The estate development is not a good place for you, Father Barrett. It is one that should be avoided."

"And why is that?"

"It's not advisable. Further involvement in the affairs of Spirit Ranch could prove extremely unfortunate for you."

"More threats." Barrett looked around. "What have you done with my dog?"

"The Spirit Ranch development is a sensitive subject for many reasons. There are many powerful—and, may I say, *ancient*—forces with a vested interest in the place. Where such powers and forces exist, there are secrets. It is not wise to involve oneself in other people's secrets, Father Barrett."

Barrett considered this and allowed his ire to deflate

somewhat. "I have no interest in your secrets," he said calmly. "I…"

Another door, this one at the far end of the room, swung open. The room beyond was lit and Barrett glimpsed the form of a…

Is that a child?

Yes, it was. Undoubtedly. A slender boy, perhaps eight, still possessing the almost feminine delicacy of early boyhood. He was barefoot and clothed in red cloth that draped his delicate shoulders like a toga. Barrett watched as he stood there in the light, staring back until a hand—an *adult* hand—reached out and fell on the boy's shoulder.

Then the door closed again.

Barrett had been on the point of saying *I'm only interested in finding two missing children* but thought the better of it.

"I…I have no interest in your secrets. Or in interfering in anything related to the development. I was asked to go there by Sergeant Lewis."

"Why?"

"He wanted my opinion on a case he's working. A missing person's case, as I recall. Might have been a First Nations…I don't remember that side of it. It was more just crime-scene review. Wanted my opinion on ingress and egress, review the evidence and—"

"Why would he ask a *priest?*"

"I used to be a police officer. Toronto. Six years as a general duty patrolman." Barrett swallowed. "Lewis and I are friends. We drink together, share news and help each other out from time to time."

"And how has Sergeant Lewis of the RCMP helped you out lately, father?"

The question surprised Barrett. He had expected his

kidnappers' interest to be the inverse—about how Barrett helped Lewis. He thought for a moment. His relationship with the sergeant was pretty one-way, with the priest receiving policeman's pay for his services on a case. He hadn't ever actually asked Lewis for help, so he improvised.

"Sergeant Lewis is not a parishioner, but he has donated money to our church and supports some of our programs. Like, for example, with the homeless. We pack sack lunches. He's helped when members of our congregation have had scrapes with the law—"

"Like in November when you smashed up Randy Jones in the Junction and wound up in jail overnight. Randy Jones, who went to the hospital and later died."

Barrett stopped breathing. That event had been his introduction to Lewis, who had declined to press charges in light of the fact that Barrett had stepped in to stop Randy from beating up a woman. The whole thing had been kept just between themselves. But somehow these guys knew.

"As you can see, father, we like to know who is in our area, and we keep an eye on them. We know about your violence. And the considerable amount of money you spend at the local liquor store buying boxes of wine. Something like two per week, isn't it? Have you spoken to anyone about your drinking?"

"That wine is for sacramental use."

"I see." The hooded man paused. "Consider this a warning, father. Stay away from the housing development. Don't pry into it by way of investigation. Keep out of the conflict between the developers and the local tribe. Find somewhere else to walk your dog."

"Alright." Barrett blinked. "Message received and understood."

With that, the hooded man withdrew and two others stepped forward. One put a breathable bag over Barrett's head while the other loosed the cuff from around the couch and refastened it to Barrett's left wrist. Then, bent over, with one man's hand on the scruff of his neck and the other holding the cuffs, he was moved out of the room double-time. Barrett was familiar with the tactic.

Russian prison guards transport maximum security prisoners this way. He had learned about it in a police academy training video. But something told him these guys weren't Russians. *They're probably the security guys for whoever owns this big house we're moving through,* he thought. A guy like that could afford to hire ex-police and military for top dollar. These guys handled themselves like soldiers. Barrett guessed Green Berets or Army Delta, or their church equivalent, the Order of St. Adrian. Barrett had worked with them on a few assignments during his time with the Curia.

Guys like this have no sense of humor whatsoever...

He was hustled down a hallway, then through a door to a stairwell. Their footsteps clattered in concrete vastness during descent. When they reached the bottom, what sounded like a heavy steel door swung open and suddenly they were outside. Barrett could hear crickets, feel the crunch of gravel underfoot and then the *crump* of a van door opening. Barrett was pushed upward and guided into a seat. *Crump!* The door was shut and the vehicle started.

They pulled out of wherever they were quickly. Barrett thought it might be a country road, but it was incredibly smooth. They were in some community somewhere? A housing development like Spirit Ranch, only complete?

Or a large private estate...

But then they were turning corners and stopping at stop lights. And then the van braked and one of the men was pulling him out onto what felt like asphalt. He was spun around, the cuffs unlocked and the daw-string tie at the bag's throat loosened.

Then something sharp and hard *(a shoe heel, likely)* smashed into the back of his calf and a man was body-checking him to the ground. As he rolled to all fours, he heard the van start up and yanked off the bag in time to see it driving away, its tail-lights blinking in the early dawn.

Have I been out almost a whole day?

He rose and looked around, recognizing the south end of Crowley Street. He was on the outskirts of the industrial zone on the north end of town, a grubby, run-down area of strip joints, diners, garages. A block up was Avro Lane, home to the Lilac Acres trailer park. His case involving Mick Hudson's missing daughter Jackie had ended there. But that day, he had had a car. It was a brief drive using the parish Hyundai, but a bit of a hike on foot.

Overhead, the sun was rising on a new day in Fulton. Barrett shaded his eyes to peer into its glow, then yanked Ray-Bans from his pocket and pushed them on.

Better get moving.

He struck off up the street.

Palaver

A CHILL SWEPT the street as Barrett walked, causing him to tighten his muscles and pull his jacket in close around his shoulders. He wondered, as he reached the intersection of Crowley and the town's main street, why there was always a chill around dawn. Barrett assumed there was some reasonable scientific explanation—something having to do with ambient temperature and sunlight, or something like that. Scientific explanations provided the *how* but rarely a *why* for the multitude of inconvenience with which the universe burdens Man. Barrett figured that's the job of religion.

I wonder what the hell they did with the dog? Barrett patted his pockets until he found cigarettes and lit one. It proved only a temporary distraction. He couldn't imagine that band of hooded psychopaths dognapping Asshole for use as a ritual sacrifice victim. He failed that test on aesthetic grounds alone. No doubt the spectre of such a critter slobbering and farting all over their Satanic trappings was one to fill even the heartiest devil worshipper with dread. But Barrett couldn't shake the fear that the mutt was lost or lying in a ditch somewhere after a close encounter with an automobile.

Well, at least I'd be rid of him then! Barrett thought. But without conviction. He set his eyes on the sidewalk ahead, puffing his coffin nail with frustration. Why the hell had he agreed to care for the damn dog in the first place? Things had been going so well. Now here he was feeling *sorry* for the thing. And guilty for imagining the worst. He figured he would alert Walton so the Conservation Officer could keep his eyes open. The dog might turn up down the road. *You just never know.*

He saw the spire of the church ahead and bent his steps that way. Fulton already showed the early stirrings of life as it came awake. Cars were pulling into McBride's parking lot. A shopkeeper swept the walk outside his door. The woman who delivered the *Tattler* to its free pick-up boxes around town was hauling a stack of issues from the rear of her hatchback. Barrett passed the church and turned the corner to the street where he lived.

An indistinct figure was bent over something on his porch. As he approached, Barrett recognized the Chief. Then, a moment later, the creature at his feet.

Asshole! Barrett muffled his sudden elation. He couldn't allow himself to be *that* pleased to see the mutt.

"That's a good dog you've got there, father." The Chief straightened with a grin. "He managed to find his way home without you."

"Been here long?" Barrett thumped up the porch steps, fumbling in his pocket for keys.

"Not long." The Chief stared down at Asshole. "He was waiting when I arrived."

Miss Dolan appeared briefly in the window then vanished, no doubt searching for some way to take offense at what she'd seen.

"Come on in and have some breakfast." Barrett held open the door and stood aside with a smile.

"Don't mind if I do." The Chief went ahead and waited in the entryway. "Only had a cup of coffee so far today."

"Well, you're in luck. Oh, Miss Dolan?" He spoke as she appeared in the kitchen doorway. "Could you set another plate for the Chief, here? And get As—I mean *the dog*—some water?"

She frowned. "Yes, father," she said crisply, and turned on her heel.

"She's a real ray of sunshine, that one." Barrett sighed. "You're up early."

"I'm always up early. To pray." He smiled. "And to pay visits on our local clergy. I hope I'm not intruding."

"Not at all, Chief." Barrett led the way to the kitchen table, where Miss Dolan was setting out another place. "I find myself, for various reasons, up early, too." He waited until Miss Dolan had served up breakfast and withdrawn before continuing. "So what brings you my way?"

"I'm just keeping in touch with you guys about our missing kids. Sergeant Lewis is helpful on the investigation side. But as a priest I think you can understand a bit more about the emotional side for us. A lot of the Otter People aren't taking this very well."

"No, I suppose not." Barrett buttered his toast. "You have a small band. Close knit. Your people feel under threat. It's unacceptable."

"We have residential school survivors in our community," said the Chief. "The pattern of having children suddenly go missing from families—of families torn apart—this raises bad memories in the people."

"I didn't know residential schools had affected your tribe."

"They affected many tribes." The Chief blinked behind his thick-framed glasses. "In the past twenty, thirty years, a lot of people have only just started remembering how to be Indians. The schools took that away from us." He paused and stared down at the table. "You know, the nearest residential school was run by people from your church. The Roman Catholics."

Barrett listened.

"When I was a kid, the RCMP came. They took me and my brother and six other kids from our village. Brought us to the residential school. I lived there for two years before I ran away. A lot of kids did. They ended up bad places. Alcoholism. The street. Or worse."

"Another bad memory being dredged up."

"It is."

They ate in silence for the next few minutes. Barrett wondered what nightmares the Chief carried around with him, and what kind of mischief he got up to after running away from the school. Had he become one of those urban Natives that hung out around places like Hastings Street in Vancouver? Or had he perhaps fallen into a life of crime and spent time in prison? Either way, he had somehow found his way back. Not many were so lucky.

Something bonked against the swinging door. Barrett looked up. The bonk came again and the door bellied slightly from its jamb. With a third, strong *bonk,* Asshole succeeded in pushing the door open and entering the kitchen. He immediately sat at Barrett's feet and gazed up with a plaintive look.

"Oh, for God sake…" Barrett knifed a slice of bacon in half and dropped it on the floor. Asshole immediately lunged over and began snuffling it down.

The Chief chuckled quietly but said nothing.

"The traditional territory of your people." Barrett chose the words for his question carefully. "Mostly the outskirts of town? The area around Fulton?"

"That. And part of the town, too." The Chief nodded in the direction of downtown. "We own the property McLellan's sits on. The police station, too. The town leases it from us. Fifty- and one-hundred-year contracts. We collect the property taxes."

Barrett raised his eyebrows. Property taxes on the downtown core would net the tribe a pretty penny on a yearly basis.

"And the housing development? The Spirit Ranch?" Barrett watched the Chief as he spoke. "Did—or, *does* —your land encompass that?"

"Do you know why it's called Spirit Ranch?"

"No." Barrett put down his knife and fork and lifted his coffee.

"The original name for the place was a nonsense word. Didn't make any sense. That's because it was the white man's version of an Indian word. Words from our language used to name the place. We used to call it Spirit Hill."

"Is that significant?"

"It is because it's where we once used to bury our dead." The Chief had stopped eating. "We always buried them there. Ever since I was a boy. The funeral processions would go up the back of the hill to the graves up top. The last one I remember was right before the RCMP came to get me. But when I returned, many years later, the land had been seized by the government."

"Seized? They didn't offer compensation?"

"No. They said the original boundaries of the reserve were wrong. That in the age of satellites and computers, they could be more accurate. I guess those computers don't much like Indians because the next thing we know, they're shaving off bits of land here and there. Including Spirit Hill. They put a fence up. It was there for many years. And then one day the fence came down and the land went up for sale." He shrugged. "We didn't have enough money at the time to buy it. So McLellan did."

"How long ago was this?"

"About fifteen years." The Chief poked at his eggs. "Years before you got here, father."

"What happened to the land then?"

"Nothing." The Chief shrugged. "It sat. For years. About eight years back, some of the tribal elders got together and we had a ceremony on the hill. Welcoming the Spirits there back into our care. Like they had been separated from us in a foreign country. Which they had."

Barrett smiled. It was a nice sentiment.

"The next summer, the surveyors appeared and the building stakes began to go up. I approached Mr. McLellan's office and requested a meeting. He agreed to see me. He explained that he had invested in a property development plan and that they were surveying the hill for estate housing. I told him about our concerns. At first, he seemed very understanding and sympathetic. He said the plans were in very preliminary stages and that he wanted to continue talking with me. At first I was optimistic."

"Then what happened?"

"We met a handful of times over the next year. Meanwhile, the bulldozers came and work began on the estate. When I asked what happened to his interest in our concerns, he said he had never made any promises to halt development and that he was under no obligation to share information with us that wasn't directly related to our conversation."

"So what did you do?"

The Chief smiled. "We went to the government of Canada and had the land revalued."

Barrett whistled. "So the government came in and gave a valuation higher than what McLellan had paid?"

"He fought it in court. But he lost." The Chief finished his coffee and stood. "He ended up having to produce another ten million dollars. The court fight and the revaluation held him up for two years but he got things back on track four years back. So we filed our lawsuit three years ago. It's pending in provincial superior court." The Chief tipped his hat. "Thanks for breakfast. And for listening."

Barrett stood. "Anytime."

———

A LINGERING discomfort nagged him for the rest of the morning. He retreated to his basement office and tried working on a sermon but it proved difficult to focus. He paused when Miss Dolan appeared at the top of the stairs to tell him his lunch was ready and he went up and ate. Miss Dolan finished for the day before he was done. He waited until she had driven away before pulling down the wine box over the sink. He shook it experimentally before pouring.

Half empty. He reminded himself to pick up a fresh one in the morning.

He took a full mug downstairs and then finished his sermon. As usual, the booze added a little extra zip to his liturgical imagery. He saved it to the hard drive and sat back, suddenly drowsy.

Half a glass and already nodding off, he thought. *I'm becoming a cheap date in my old age.*

Passages

BARRETT DROWSED, coming awake periodically to tinker with his sermon and surf the internet before heading upstairs for a refill. Then he returned to his office and sat at his desk, the wine fogging his awareness such that he cycled through the stages of wakefulness, drowsiness and a light sleep in a seamless pattern. One led to the other until he could no longer tell the difference between dream and memory, and between things recollected from the past or exaggerated by his unconscious mind.

It's the damn booze, he thought. *It's breaking up my sleep patterns.*

He sipped. And drowsed. And remembered…

———

HIS PAST. It always came back down to that. Of an average day, Barrett wouldn't think about it much, preferring to suppress memories of the large, dark house he shared with his mother and father during his uncomfortable childhood, of the piano in the front room beneath which he took refuge in moments of anguish or crisis. He had been there as a boy on the night his father shot a man *(murderer)* and disposed of the body with the help of friends, the same serious, quiet men in dark suits who came and went. These same men appeared at cocktail parties, wives on their arms, to ape the convivial habits of the wealthy and powerful. Barrett had known, even as a boy, that his family and their friends did not legitimately belong to the upper class. They had simply staked a claim there as a result of having money. Barrett wondered if resentment played a role in the massive violence with which they had staked that claim.

His father used to run "errands." Barrett had heard the term in school, associating it with the usual connotations of grocery, post-office, dry cleaners. But by the time he was eight, he recognized these "errands" occurred with a regularity that set them apart from typical household needs. His father was going to collect something—something that could not be bagged at a cash register or wrapped in a package.

He was nine the day his father came to collect him from school. Barrett remembered it was winter, and that he had been forced to wait until it was dark and all the other kids had gone home before his lift arrived. A teacher had arrived with a note from the office. His mother was sick so his father was coming but would be delayed. So Barrett had waited in the locker room until he arrived.

A horn honked outside the locker room door—loud and insistent. Barrett had risen, gathering his schoolbag and jacket, and stepped out into the swirling snow, crossing the cold, dark distance from the school to his father's Lincoln. His father didn't look at him as he got in.

"Be sure to put your seatbelt on," dad said. "I have a stop to make downtown before we head home. Shouldn't take too long."

Barrett was cold, tired and hungry. But he knew better than to argue with his father. So he steeled himself for a delayed dinner.

The Lincoln pulled away from the school and into the flow of traffic headed downtown. Barrett watched as the familiar neighborhood of the school gave way to government and office buildings. He saw the high rise in which his father maintained an office and was surprised when the car drove right past and kept on going. He opened his mouth to ask why but sensed his father's mood was dark. Dad wasn't in the vein for answering questions. He knew the signs.

At length, his father turned into a crowded, dingy neighborhood where pedestrians outnumbered vehicles. Barrett noted the profusion of signs in foreign languages. He knew enough to distinguish Hindu lettering from Oriental, but not enough to distinguish Chinese from Japanese. After a while, he decided it must be Chinese because of the establishments he passed. He recognized pictures of items he associated with the Chinese immigrants to Toronto—dry cleaning and boutique grocery establishments, and restaurants like the one they parked beside.

"You stay here," his father said. "I—"

Then his father stopped and squinted through the window. A figure was making his way down the sidewalk toward them. Barrett recognized the distinct silhouette of a city policeman.

"Never mind." Dad snatched the keys from the ignition. "Come with me. Be sure to lock the door behind you."

Barrett did as he was told.

———

BARRETT'S HEAD drooped until his chin was on his chest. The pain in his neck woke him. He pushed away the memories of the winter, the Lincoln, his father. And wondered at the tightness knotting his gut. He rose and shuffled upstairs for a refill.

The house was dark and cold. Miss Dolan had turned down the heat when she left. Barrett found the thermostat, turned up the temperature and returned to the wine box where he had left it sitting by the kitchen sink. He uttered a grumble of satisfaction as the heater groaned to life, pushing tired, warm air into the kitchen. Growing up in Toronto had meant cold and lengthy winters. Sub-zero was the norm. He had acclimatized to rainforest BC with its milder temperatures and rare island snowfall. His blood had thinned and he had learned to fear the cold.

He made his way back downstairs carefully, clutching the banister lest he stumble and spill wine. He returned to his desk.

He did not want to remember more. He wanted to focus on his adult life—his parish duties, his occasional investigative work for Lewis, his place in the community (such as it was). But the wine was breaking down more than just the barrier between drowsiness and sleep, between sleep and wakefulness. It was breaking down his ability to push away painful memories.

I haven't eaten Chinese food in years, he realized. The realization hit him like a brick. He wondered, sipping, why that was. For he had always found Chinese food delicious. Ever since he was a kid…

———

BARRETT FOLLOWED his father into the restaurant. It was dark and empty. The white circles of unoccupied tables draped in cheap cloth marched toward the service counter to the kitchen. The hostess podium and cash register by the door remained unoccupied, undulating in the glowing light from the fish tank by the door. Three fat goldfish swam boredly in its greenish water.

The swinging door to the kitchen opened and a short, slender Chinese man in an apron bustled out, pausing to grab two menus from the counter before hurrying over.

"Sorry, sorry," he said, chuckling, eyes on the menus he held as he approached. He was still smiling when he looked up and caught sight of Barrett's father. Then the smile plummeted.

"Hello, Yi." Barrett's father spoke in his most serious tone, the one Barrett associated with punishment. He knew this restaurant. His family had eaten here before. And every time, his father had addressed the owner as "Mr. Yi."

But not tonight.

"Ah, Mr. Barrett. Hello." Yi's arm dropped, the menus dangling from one hand. "I have been trying to call you—"

"I've been in the office all day. Like I was yesterday and the day before."

"Ah. I have been unable to get through…"

"That's why I sent Jerry down to have a talk with you."

"So you did. I—"

"Let's step into the back and have a talk." The way Barrett's father smiled when he said this brooked no argument.

Mr. Yi conducted them back to the kitchen. Barrett's father turned and flicked off the neon OPEN sign in the window, then locked the front door before following. Barrett, fear seizing his guts, trailed behind.

He saw the door to the kitchen swing wide, throwing a block of light into the room. It dazzled his eyes, so he shaded them as he passed through into the long, empty kitchen. A table at its center was crowded with boxes of dried goods, discarded newspapers and full ashtrays. A large pot bubbled fitfully on a nearby stove.

"So." Barrett's father planted himself before Yi, arms crossed. "What's the problem?"

"Ah, no problem." Mr. Yi gave a watery smile. "I just need more time…"

"Your time is up, Mr. Yi. You owe us. Now we have an arrangement. In exchange for our services, you pay a fee. That fee is collected monthly by my associates. For the past few months, that's been Jerry."

"Ah, yes. Mr. Jerry…" Yi's smile faltered again. "When he came in, he—"

"When he came in you failed to pay him." Barrett's father stepped forward. "You said you needed a week. He returned a second time and still you did not pay him. So I've come. Mr. Yi. I don't appreciate having to come down to discharge a duty that could just as easily have been handled by one of my associates."

"Yes."

"You're wasting my time, understand?"

"Y—yes."

"So." Barrett's father smiled. "Now that that's all

cleared up, you can pay me what you owe and we'll be square."

"Ah. Yes." Yi looked lost. "Mr. Barrett, I—"

"That's two hundred and fifty dollars."

"Yes. I—"

"*You* will pay it."

"No, I—"

"WHAT?"

The hairs on the back of Barrett's neck stood on end. The tone was a louder version of the one Barrett recognized from incidents which had ended with him getting smacked.

Now his father was moving, stepping forward with that angry, determined step Barrett knew so well—the urgent stride with which his father answered challenges to his authority. He grasped Yi's left arm at the wrist and dragged him toward the pot bubbling on the stove top.

"No!" Yi struggled, straining to pull away. "Mr. Barrett! No!"

Barrett watched as his father maneuvered Yi's arm by the elbow and began sinking the hand into the boiling liquid in the pot. Yi's expression went from pale to bright red as the dam of fear broke into absolute pain and terror. Barrett's father was stronger and bigger than the Chinese man. His face was impassive as he held Yi's arm, nearly elbow-deep, in the boiling fluid until he passed out. Barrett turned away and closed his eyes as the man hit the floor.

Barrett did not breathe through the long silence that followed, remaining perfectly still until his father's hand touched his shoulder.

"Come on, son," he said tiredly. "Let's go home."

———

BARRETT STARTED AWAKE. His wine was empty and the house was quiet. His bleary expression stared back at him from the darkened computer screen. He pushed himself upright and plucked his mug from the desk, shambling upstairs. There was a knot behind his eyes and a thick fog clouding his thoughts.

What the hell time is it? he wondered.

The wine box was distressingly light when he lifted it. How much had he had to drink? At some point in the night he had lost count. He decided to take it easy and only pour himself part of a mug before putting the box away. He turned and leaned against the sink, sipping. His eyes found the digital clock on the stove.

2:58 AM.

A wave of nausea coursed through his guts. He paused drinking long enough to swallow it down and steady himself.

I have to cut down on this stuff, he thought, examining the wine in his mug. It was a thought that had occurred to him only about a hundred times before. When he wondered why he couldn't, he flashed on a memory of Mr. Yi's hand being lowered into the pot of boiling liquid…

Stop it!

Barrett swigged down the last of his wine, switched off the kitchen light and made for the bedroom. He was halfway there when the phone rang.

Barrett answered from the extension on the hall table. "Hello?" he asked.

"Hello, padre," said Lewis. "I'm up at the hospital. One of our missing Native kids has turned up."

Barrett raised his eyebrows. "I'll be right there," he promised, and hung up.

Sleep Of Reason

HE PULLED into the ambulance bay of the hospital and parked beside Lewis' patrol car. The charge nurse, seeing he was clergy, just waved him through the reception area and straight into the ER waiting room. Lewis, his craggy face drawn in a tangle of exhaustion, looked up from his seat and ran a hand through his thick gray hair.

"Heya, padre." He stood. "Thanks for coming."

"Is it Sabrina? Or Jason?"

"It's Jason Joe." Lewis led them down a low-ceilinged corridor that was half-lit in the pre-dawn stillness. "He's unconscious and they've got him under observation and in ICU. Here."

Lewis pushed open a swinging door marked INTENSIVE CARE—NO VISITORS. A small antechamber beyond led into the darkened cavern of the ICU patient care room. A lone nurse filled out paper-work at a desk. Barrett saw four beds, three of which were empty. In the fourth lay Jason Joe.

Barrett recognized him from town. He was a young teen of perhaps 13 years. The kid was usually to be found skateboarding around downtown—a pleasant, slightly chubby kid in a Canucks ballcap with a ready smile and infectious laugh. Sort of a joker, but generally not a bad sort. The contrast between that image and the form lying under hospital sheets could not have been more stark. The kid's normally round face was slack and drawn. He had lost weight. Barrett thought he saw bruises on the boy's neck and shoulders.

Lewis spoke, his voice tight. "I got a call from Max Simpson, the property caretaker. He was returning home at 1 AM after a trip down-island and spotted the boy wandering the streets of Spirit Ranch, delirious. He called us and BC Ambulance Service. They attended and picked him up. He fell unconscious on the drive to the hospital."

The nurse was up now, approaching them with a clipboard in hand.

"Hi, Gavin. Father." The nurse was older up close than she first appeared. Barrett watched her drag reading glasses from her scrubs and perch them on her nose. "Jason is a very lucky young man. He was seriously dehydrated. Electrolytes scrambled like a batch of eggs Florentine. Hasn't eaten in days. There's some indication of trauma, likely inflicted by blows or rough handling. He came back from X-rays a half-hour ago." She flipped a page on her clipboard. "No broken bones, no immediate evidence of internal damage. But he's definitely been starved and roughed up. Continuously over a period of time. We're doing an MRI tomorrow morning."

"Thanks, Jenelle." Lewis smiled as she drifted over to check the equipment monitoring the boy. "So the kid's been beaten."

"He's not the only one."

Lewis' eyes narrowed. "What are you talking about?"

"I was poking around Spirit Ranch and somebody cold-cocked me." Barrett's hands drifted to his pockets. He was desperate for a cigarette. "I woke up in a room full of men who threatened me. Said I needed to keep away from Spirit Ranch and 'other people's secrets.'"

"Did you recognize any of them?"

"I couldn't. They…" Barrett hesitated to say it. "They were all wearing robes."

"*Robes?*" A confused half-smile twisted Lewis' mouth. "What? You mean, like, *bathrobes?*"

"No. Um, more like… Monk's robes. But black. And hooded. And—"

"Wait a minute." Lewis held up a hand. "You mean to tell me a bunch of robed and hooded men threatened you?"

"There was a knife," Barrett added. "And…candles. It was weird. Had a kind of a ritual, Satanic vibe to it."

Lewis said nothing for a long moment. Then he opened his mouth to speak, appeared to reconsider and closed it again.

"What?" Barrett was growing impatient.

"Padre…" Lewis sighed. "Do you have any idea how ridiculous that sounds? *'A pack of Satanists kidnapped me and told me not to visit the housing development.'* I mean, that would be far-fetched. Even for a novel."

"*IT HAPPENED, GAVIN!*"

"*Where* did it happen?"

"I don't know. They zip-tied my wrists and put a bag over my head. Car trip there. Car trip back. I…I have no idea."

"Did they injure you?"

"No." Barrett rubbed his wrist. "Just kinda' roughed

me up a bit. I…" Barrett struggled to remember. "I think I saw a kid there."

"A *kid?*" Lewis's mouth tightened into a frown. "What? You mean…in robes? As part of the…"

"No. The kid was only partially dressed."

Lewis gaped.

"He was only visible for a second. Then a hand reached for him. And a door closed. And…" Barrett trailed off.

"Okay. Okay," Lewis offered quietly. "Let me see what I can dig up in our files about occult crime. I've got to say…in my time here, I've encountered almost no trace of it in Fulton. But you never know." He paused. "It's certainly compelling, though. And could very well play into Jason's case. Any group sick enough to kidnap and threaten a priest almost certainly wouldn't hesitate to do the same to a kid."

"Yeah. That's what I'm thinking."

Lewis turned to gaze down at the prone form of the boy. "I still haven't had a chance to interview Simpson. You want to handle that for me?" He smirked. "Assuming you're not afraid of trespassing on the estate and encountering more wrath from robed men…"

"Oh, no." Barrett's hand curled into a fist. "Nothing I'd like better than to corner one of those bastards and ring his bell. Hard."

———

BARRETT RETURNED to the parish house in time to get breakfast from Miss Dolan.

"Where've you been getting to, father?" she asked, putting a plate of scrambled eggs down before him.

"You've been staying out late, coming home at ungodly hours."

"Pastoral duties," he said vaguely. "Do we still have tabasco sauce?"

"No, father. I stopped buying that. It's not good for you."

"But I *like* it. The same way I like cigarettes and wine. Miss Dolan, would you *please* pick up a jar of tabasco sauce next time you go shopping?"

"Many of the bottles have devils depicted on them, father."

"Fine." He forked up a clutch of egg. "Buy one that doesn't have a devil on the label. If that will make you feel better."

She appeared relieved. "It would, father."

"Great. I appreciate your diligence in keeping my pantry Christian."

"Oh, it's my duty, father. No need to thank me," she said, and shambled off to dust the living room.

As Barrett ate, Asshole shambled into the room and plunked himself down on his ass at Barrett's feet. Barrett looked down in disgust.

"Stupid dog," he said absently, breaking off part of his toast and dropping it before his paws. Barrett watched as it vanished in the blink of an eye, certain the bulldog must routinely set some sort of land speed record for eating.

Barrett went down to his office to do some paperwork and answer a few e-mails. Around 9 AM, he leashed up Asshole and walked to the church, doing a circuit of the building to the rear lot where an aging RV moldered beneath the drooping branches of the trees at the edge of the property. The RV had been there so long it seemed to be every bit as attached to the ground as the flora itself. Barrett knocked on the door and waited until it opened.

"Heya, father," said Scooter. The groundskeeper's thin, unshaven face poked out beneath the brim of his ballcap. "How's tricks?"

"Fine, Scooter. Listen. I was wondering if you'd mind dog-sitting for a few hours. I have some errands to run."

"Dog?" Scooter peered down at Asshole. "Miss Doyle said something about you getting a dog. That him?"

"Yeah." Barrett sighed. "And he's not really *my* dog. He was just sort of...*left behind* by Edith Anderson when she went to assisted living. I'm taking care of him until... Say. *You* wouldn't be interested in having him, by any chance? Would you?"

"Permanently? No. I got no room in here." Scooter smiled. "But I'll take him for a few hours, sure. What's his name?"

"Uh, he doesn't have one. Not really, anyway."

"Well, what did Mrs. Anderson call him?"

"Princess Woogums."

Scooter blinked. "Yeah. Sounds like she was ready for the nuthatch, alright. Leave him with me, father. I'll take care of him 'til you get back."

———

A PHALANX of storm clouds marched across the sun as Barrett strode into the housing development. Although the drop in temperature was mild, he nevertheless shivered and pulled his jacket more tightly around his shoulders. Rain always reminded him of his youth, of those years he took refuge beneath the piano to avoid his father's violence and rages.

I'm in my forties, Barrett thought. *Should be over all that childhood shit by now.*

He stuffed the thoughts down, congratulating himself on exhibiting mental discipline. Then he checked his watch and reminded himself he only had to wait another hour or so and before he could have his first drink of the day.

He turned a corner into a street of finished houses. He was wondering how he would find Max when the caretaker appeared in the doorway of one home, carrying a toolbox. Barrett watched as he let himself out, carefully locking the door behind him before turning to leave.

"Mr. Simpson!" Barrett waved and jogged over. "Hello. How are you?"

"Father Barrett! Hi!" Max shifted the toolbox to his left hand and stuck out his right. "Where's your dog?"

"Uh, he's not my dog." Barrett shook. "I left him with a friend. Max, do you have a moment to talk?"

"Sure, padre. Come on follow me to my car." He hefted the toolbox. "This thing is heavy."

"Sure thing." Barrett followed Max around to the back of the house and through the yard of the one behind it to the next street where a gleaming, low-slung sportscar sat at the curb. "Wow!" he exclaimed, eyebrows lifting. "Nice wheels, Max."

"Ha. Thanks, father." Max slid his keys out of his pocket and opened the narrow trunk, which rose like a hatch on the starship Enterprise. "It's a Lamborghini Huracán."

"I didn't know they paid caretakers that well!"

Max laughed as he put the toolbox in the trunk and closed it. "Not *that* well. No, father. I've always been a car guy. That's my passion. If you love something enough, well..." He reached out and stroked the

Lambo's roof. "I guess you're willing to scrimp and save for it."

Barrett nodded. Cars like this ran in the low six figures for a price tag. "I admire your thrift," he said sincerely. "Say, I understand you're the one who found Jason Joe."

"Who?" Max looked puzzled for a moment. Then: "Oh, the Indian kid! Yeah. That was me."

"So he was wandering delirious when you found him?"

"Sure was." Max leaned on the car and looked down. "Could barely stand up. Looked like a sleepwalker."

"Did he say anything?"

"No." Max crossed his arms. "I tried to get him to talk but all I got was mumbles. He passed out when I was calling Sergeant Lewis."

"Any indication of where he might have come from?"

"No." Max seemed surprised at the question. "Could have come from anywhere."

"Where did you find him?"

"There." Max pointed. "That street in front of the house I just came out of."

"Did you notice anything peculiar about him?"

"Sure! That he was out alone at 1 AM and walking around like a zombie. That was plenty peculiar to me."

Barrett smiled. "I suppose that would be strange. Thanks for your time, Max."

"Any time, father." The caretaker shook hands and then climbed into his starship.

Barrett heard the low growl of the precision Italian engine and watched as Max motored away up the street and turned a corner. He walked back around to the front door from which Max had just emerged.

So the kid's delirious and stumbling around, Barrett

thought. *Doesn't make any sense. If he was that out of it, then how did he make his way here?*

Barrett walked out to the street and scanned the horizon. The nearest visible structure was miles away. He was identifying various landmarks in his mind when an engine sounded behind him. He turned.

A Lincoln pulled up, driven by McLellan's attorney, Stroud. He waved and braked to a stop beside Barrett.

"Father Barrett, hi. Was hoping I'd find you here." Stroud unlocked the door. "Do you have a minute? Mr. McLellan wants to see you."

Negotiation

BARRETT HESITATED. "How did you know I was here?" he asked suspiciously. The coincidence of Stroud's sudden appearance with yesterday's warning from the robed men was unsettling.

"Sergeant Lewis told me I might find you here." Stroud smiled. "I went to your house first. He drove by as I was getting back into my car. Flagged him down to ask." His brow knitted. "Say … your housekeeper's not very friendly…"

"Oh?" Barrett smirked.

"She told me it was 'bad form'," (Stroud actually mimed air quotes to this) "to appear at a priest's house without first making an appointment. She was rather brusque with me, to be honest."

"I'll have a word with her," Barrett promised, smarting slightly at the lie. He decided Stroud was on the level and pulled open the passenger side door. "How is Mr. McLellan?"

"Oh, quite recovered. Partially, anyway. Hospice released him but we expect he'll be back there soon. He's quite sick." Stroud put the car into drive and pulled from the curb as Barrett fastened his seatbelt. "Any word back from your superior on the contract?"

"None yet. I left a voicemail with his office yesterday evening," Barrett lied. "I'll let you know the moment I hear from him."

"Excellent."

Stroud guided the car through Fulton, passing the law enforcement offices and row of boutiques downtown and then turning down Crowley Street. One block before the trailer park was Flagg Street. Stroud took a right and sped up. Barrett was unfamiliar with this area outside of town. The street ran past fields and the few farms outside of town. Within a few minutes they were enclosed on all sides by forest. Barrett flashed back to his ride back into Fulton after his close encounter with the robed men.

Is it possible that…

A driveway appeared from between the trees on the right-hand side of the road. Stroud steered to follow the driveway to a tall wrought iron gate between two vast stone pillars. The attorney tapped a code into a keypad on a panel set into one of the pillars and the gates opened.

"This is Mr. McLellan's estate." Stroud drove through the gate and waited until it closed behind him to resume driving. "He ordinarily doesn't care for visitors. You're being accorded a great honor."

"I see," Barrett said sceptically. Stroud's words suggested that some expression of gratitude would be appropriate under the circumstances. It was like being nudged by your parents to say thank you after receiving a Christmas present. Barrett hated that kind of infantilizing talk, so he said nothing.

The driveway topped out onto a flat rise. There, partially concealed by old growth trees, was a huge mansion. To Barrett it resembled something from *Downton Abbey*. Tiered blocks of hewn stone rose to window casings resembling something from a Medieval castle. Copper roofing, green-tinged, buttresses and balustraded balconies, it was every inch the modern castle in form and function. Stroud followed a long, curving stretch of the driveway which led beneath a port cochere where a tall man in a dark suit stood waiting.

"Father. Mr. Stroud." The man nodded to them as they emerged. "Mr. McLellan is in the library."

Now I get to find out if it's the same library those robed weirdoes took me to, Barrett thought as he followed Stroud up the entryway steps to a glass and walnut entry hall. The main foyer was visible through the glass. A wide, carpeted staircase dominated the space, its bannisters filigreed with newels and scrollwork. As Barrett followed Stroud to the second floor he noted the profusion of huge, classical oil paintings adorning the walls. Mahogany side tables dominated the hallway that was inset with nooks in which loomed marble statuary. It was the sort of décor, Barrett reflected, that would look more at home in Buckingham Palace than a mansion on Vancouver Island, but McLellan had money to burn and an ego the size of British Columbia so it basically fit.

The poor aspire to be rich, the rich aspire to be royalty and royalty aspire to be gods, Barrett thought. Life at society's upper tiers was one big game of one-upmanship.

Stroud paused outside the door to the library, his hand on the knob. "I feel it fair to warn you, father. Mr. Stroud is not alone. There is a third party present."

"Who?"

In response, Stroud pushed open the door.

Nope, not the same library, Barrett thought with a relief that was short lived. Because inside the library, a vast room portioned with rows of book racks like a public library, was McLellan reclining in a padded wheelchair. And across the room from him was one of the robed men from the night Barrett was kidnapped.

———

HE STEADIED HIMSELF. The body shock accompanying the sight of the hooded man was volcanic. There came no indication from the shadow within the hood that the man recognized Barrett. But Barrett recognized him. There was no doubt he was one of those who had been in the library.

"Father Barrett." McLellan's voice was soft but audible in the large room. "Thank you for coming. I've asked you here as my spiritual advisor."

"I was glad to come, of course." Barrett looked at the robed, hooded man. "Who's your friend?"

"Allow me to introduce Frater Nox of the Black Star Temple."

"We've met. Brother Night, eh?" Barrett smirked and shook his head. *Such theatrics!* he thought. "And the Black Star Temple is?"

"An organization with which I have had some involvement, father." McLellan leaned forward slightly, eager to keep control of the proceedings. "Frater Nox is the counsel for the other side."

"I didn't know Satanists used lawyers." Barrett flicked a glance at the robe. "I thought they just sacrificed goats or whatever it is they vivisect in order to get what they want." He turned back to McLellan. "What am I doing here?"

"You remember the contract I had Stroud bring you?"

"It's under review, Mr. McLellan."

"Good. Good." McLellan addressed Frater Nox. "As a signatory to our agreement, I am pressing for the right to amend the agreement with a codicil. You can see I am unwell. The doctors tell me I don't have much time. I have my attorney and my spiritual counsellor present. Father Barrett is attending me in hospice, you see."

The hooded man finally spoke. "Your impending death changes nothing, McLellan." He reached into his robe and produced a scroll, which spilled open when he cast it on a nearby table. "You signed the Contract. There is no proviso to amend it. Quid pro quo. We gave to you. And you, in your turn, will give to us."

Stroud stepped over and lifted the document from the table, steadying it with the practiced gestures of a man who spends the majority of his life absorbed in paperwork. He looked down at the print for a long moment before turning to McLellan.

"I can't read this," he said. "It's in a foreign language."

"It's Latin. That's why I had you bring Father Barrett." McLellan adjusted his position in the wheel-chair. "Let him take a look."

Stroud stepped over to Barrett and offered the document. It was a long parchment with a brass cylinder at each end, the sort of thing you'd see used as a prop in a movie about ancient Rome. Barrett accepted the scroll and rolled it open. The main text on the page was done by hand in black ink, and the signature (McLellan's) was a dull red, as if he had signed in...

Blood.

Barrett had the dimmest recollections of a dream and

felt a stirring of unease. He reapplied himself to the document.

"Okay." He sighed and began reading. A few hundred words of turgid legalese that ended with a surprise that made Barrett stop breathing for a few seconds. He looked up. "This is how you got the extra money to cover the property revaluation by the government?"

McLellan nodded.

"Well." Barrett rolled the scroll back up and addressed the hooded man. "My, my. You boys must have deep pockets. Ten million. Quite a princely sum."

"Unlike the Vatican, the Black Star Temple's assets exist in negotiable tender and are accessible for the good of humanity," said Frater Nox.

"For a price." Barrett's tone was arctic.

"Nothing is free," replied Nox.

"No shit," muttered Barrett, longing for a cigarette.

Stroud spoke up. "Father, is our learned friend here telling us the truth? Is there no proviso in there to amend or renegotiate?"

"*Termini sunt finales* is the phrase. 'These terms are final.'" He waggled the scroll. "That's what it says."

Although the hooded man did not speak and his facial expression was obscured by the hood, Barrett couldn't shake the sense of satisfaction that wafted from his robed figure.

Stroud turned to McLellan. "It seems that you sold your soul to the Devil for ten million dollars and there's no room to negotiate."

"Goddammit!" McLellan thumped the arm of his wheelchair. "What the hell do I pay you for? Get me out of this thing! Any contract is subject to review by a court of law."

"That's precisely the point, Arnold." Stroud knelt by the wheelchair and clasped McLellan's forearm. "I'm licensed to practice law in the province of BC. What court would something like this be judged in? Canadian contract law has no...*frame of reference* for this kind of thing. And besides, who would enforce the court's decision, even if it *did* go in your favor? Which is unlikely given how the language is framed."

"That's why I've asked Father Barrett here today." McLellan shifted in his seat and addressed the priest. "The Final Judgment is God's. Isn't that correct, father?"

Barrett nodded.

"There!" McLellan glared triumphantly at Stroud. "*That's* the court this gets decided in. So I have two advocates. You for BC. And Father Barrett with God. Isn't that right, father?"

"I wish you had decided you were interested in the state of your soul before you got cancer," Barrett said evenly. "If you had been under my pastoral care and asked me, I would have advised you in no uncertain terms *not* to sign this infernal thing. It's an insult to everything decent in the world." He turned to Frater Nox. "You people with your ridiculous sense of grandeur! You presume to negotiate for the Devil himself?"

Nox spoke. "Then you believe he's real, father?"

"Of course the Devil is real!" Barrett smacked his palm with a fist. "I was a general duty patrolman with the Toronto police for six years! I worked the red zone in the inner city. I watched women holding babies as they shot heroin into their arms! Watched children with gunshot wounds be loaded into the back of ambulances! Watched fathers pimp out their own daughters for crack! You can't see that kind of thing day after day and not believe evil—true evil—is real! And it has an author." He glared at Nox. "Your *boss*. You *sick* son-of-a-bitch! If we weren't in Arnold McLellan's house right now I'd *end* you."

"I thought priests took vows of nonviolence," replied Frater Nox.

"Yeah?" Barrett narrowed his eyes. "Well, even priests occasionally sin. I'll take the hit. If it means getting my hands around your throat!"

"Father. Calm down." It was McLellan's turn to smooth the waters. "You've reviewed the contract. Is there nothing in there to work with?"

"No. Not really." Barrett unrolled the document again, scanning the words. Something caught his eye. He reviewed the preamble again. "What's this?" he asked Nox, pointing to a phrase. " *'Subscriptorem vel substitute.'* Signatory or substitute."

The hood shifted. Just enough of Nox's face appeared to make his smile visible. "It is Mr. McLellan's right to offer a substitute. If he can find one."

"A substitute *what?*"

"Soul."

Confrontation

BARRETT'S DISBELIEF WAS MASSIVE, striking him like a hammer blow. He opened his mouth to cry *"What?"* when McLellan piped up and forced the conversation to a whole new level.

"Would a child's soul do?"

"Of course." Real satisfaction seemed to swell Nox's voice. "Purity is coveted above all other vices."

Barrett's head swam. He was flashing…*(child standing in the doorway across the room)*…on the image of a child standing…*(father lowering Yi's arm nearly elbow-deep, into the boiling fluid)*…in the doorway across the room and his head was swimming. But he got a hold of himself. He opened his mouth again. "Look," he said. "I –"

"Excuse me, father." McLellan flapped a hand. "Anton, why don't you and Frater Nox hammer out the details? I'll finish here with the good father."

Barrett seethed as he watched the lawyer usher the Satanist out of the room. He waited until the door clicked shut before rounding on McLellan.

"*'Would a child's soul do?'* What the hell was that supposed to mean?" Barrett was on his feet now, shaking with rage. "What kind of *horseshit* is going on here? Just how do you intend to furnish that robed freak with a child's soul?"

"Father, calm down…"

"I *will not* calm down!" Barrett was shaking his fist. "Jesus! Arnold! You engage me to be your hospice counsellor, despite not being a Catholic. You provide a massive bequest to our church, and then attempt to *bribe* the diocese into rubber stamping some half-baked contract with God. And *only now* do I come to find out you're mixed up with a bunch of Satanists and have signed a contract with Lucifer to sell your *soul?*"

McLellan sat mum.

"Arnold. Arnold! Are you a Satanist?"

McLellan sighed, exasperated. "No! I don't even believe in any of that stuff."

"What about God?" Barrett fought to rein in his rage. It was difficult. "Do you even believe in God?"

"Well…let's say I'm just hedging my bets. Like a good investment."

"*What the hell do you mean about offering them a child's soul?*"

McLellan held up his hands. "It's a saying that derives from Aleister Crowley's writings in *Liber AL vel Legis,* The Book of the Law. He speaks of a 'crowned and conquering child' as the herald of a new age. When I speak of offering a 'child's soul,' I am offering to undergo a ritual purification and dedication to their God. Strictly symbolic. By lying on a table and allowing them to burn incense and chant esoteric mumbo-jumbo over me, I undergo a symbolic death. Ridiculous, of course. But those sorts of shenanigans seem to placate them when they get difficult."

Barrett trembled, feeling at once foolish and betrayed, furious with himself for ever believing he could offer any sort of lasting spiritual counsel to a man so utterly shallow and depraved, a man who gamed religions against each other like investments, who routinely insulted and betrayed others, including members of his own family and whose personal disposition was so unpleasant that his own son could barely stand to be around him in his final hours. At length, he spoke.

"Mr. McLellan, I'm done. I'm out. I'll be pleased to direct you to other members of the clergy, but I'm finished as your hospice care religious counsellor. Find someone else."

With that, he turned on his heel and left.

———

BARRETT STALKED out of the house and down the long driveway toward the road. He probably had several hours' walk ahead of him, but he didn't care. He didn't want a ride in Stroud's car or even McLellan's chauffeured limo. He just wanted to be the hell away from that nest of freaks and egomaniacs. Hell, he didn't mind if he had to spend the night in the damn forest! Driving his fists down into his coat pockets, he set his shoulders and marched on.

I'm telling Lewis everything I know about the kids I've seen, heard about, or imagined, he thought. He also resolved to ask the Mountie to look into the Black Star Temple. The added wrinkle of occult weirdness introduced another level of danger to the proceedings. They had taught him in seminary about the overlap between occult lodges and occult crime, a truth he had confirmed years before on the police force.

We're getting closer, he thought. *Each move, closer and closer to whoever's behind the disappearance of those kids.*

He wondered how Jason Joe was doing in the hospital. Reaching the road, he grappled out his cellphone, and thumbed the power button. He still had 75% of his battery but no cell signal out this far. He jammed the phone back in a pocket and pulled cigarettes from another. For a few minutes he just stood smoking at the shoulder of the road across from McLellan's driveway, absorbing everything he'd experienced. He was still standing there when the sound of a Harley roared in the distance.

It was a sound Barrett had come to know well during his last spell of investigating for Lewis. At the time, he'd owed Lewis a favor, the Mountie having pulled his ass from the fire by declining to press charges on an assault Barrett had committed. The ensuing chain of events had drawn Barrett into close contact with Mick Hudson and the Paladins and so he greeted the sound with a kind of relief.

You know you've crossed into a different country when a Harley's engine sounds like safety, he thought. And marvelled at the island's weird social ecosystem.

A lone figure appeared in the distance—a man astride a booming Harley. Soon he was braking to a halt beside Barrett. Beneath the shades and bandana, Barrett recognized Big Mick. The biker's presence out this way was no surprise. Mick's compound was also rural and his crew often used the unpatrolled logging roads as their preferred migration routes. With one gloved hand, Mick downshifted the engine to a growling purr.

"Hey, father. You need a lift into town?"

"Sure do."

"Hop on."

Barrett swung a leg over the Harley's back seat and felt the bike howl to life beneath him as Mick repositioned himself over the handlebars and resumed course. For a few minutes, the route seemed familiar to Barrett. But then Mick steered off a side road and slowed to speak back over his shoulder.

"Got a stop to make on the way, father. Not too far out of the way. Perhaps an extra fifteen minutes."

"No problem."

Mick's detour was a narrow, winding, hard-packed dirt road. More stable and kempt than your average logging road. Barrett guessed it was probably used by utility companies repairing electrical substations out this way. After a few minutes, Mick crested the top of a hill and pulled over beside a squat metallic structure.

"It's a portable work shelter," Mick said, switching off the bike and dismounting. "They come with a hook up for water and propane, a dining area and a bathroom if you need to use it, father."

"No, I'm fine, thanks." Barrett got off the bike and stretched. He watched as Mick stepped over to the door of the shelter and produced a key which opened the hatch inset on the structure's side. Barrett marvelled at the high-tech simplicity of the idea. It was the sort of thing the power company could easily drop in here by helicopter. He pulled out cigarettes and was just preparing to light up when Mick emerged with a backpack over his shoulder. Without looking at Barrett, he stepped over and unloaded its contents furtively into a saddlebag, then squashed the pack up and pushed it in after. He strolled over to Barrett, pulling a joint out from behind his ear. He lit it up and took a few puffs before offering it to the priest. Barrett took a few puffs just to be polite.

"Say, Mick," Barrett said after a few minutes. "Do you know about any occult groups in the area?"

"Oh-cult?" Mick frowned, puzzled. "What, you mean like witchcraft and Satanism and like that? Nah." He shook his head, paused and thought for a minute, then resumed shaking it even harder. "Not around here. There *was* this motorcycle gang in Campbell River for a while, Los Guerreros. Mexican guys. Nice guys, we never had a problem with 'em. They had some o' that going on. But they're not around anymore."

"What happened to them?"

"Gang just sort of fell apart." Mick shrugged. "There just weren't enough of them to keep the club going. They were the only oh-cult thing around here I ever heard about." He sucked on the joint and paused to scratch his head. "Them and Squatch. You know about Squatch?"

"The one who skulks in the woods and steals soap from people's bathrooms?" Barrett recalled his own rectory break in.

"Yeah." Mick chuckled. "That's him. Anyway, he's got another nickname. Kokopeli. Like the desert legend about the guy with the flute and the sack on his back? They call him Kokopeli because anytime anyone's ever caught a glimpse of him, he's always been carrying this huge duffle on his back. He's a big fucker, too. Like, more than six-five. Isn't Kokopeli kind of occult?"

"I guess." Barrett didn't bother asking about the Black Star Temple.

MICK DROPPED him at the church. Barrett thanked him and went into his office. A stack of mail was waiting in his inbox. It took him two hours to clear it and, just when he was getting ready to leave, a parishioner showed up that was in need of some urgent counsel. Barrett brought her into the church and sat with her for two hours, listening and advising her through a family loss. By the time he was done, he was exhausted. After seeing her out, he took a seat on the couch in his office to rest and dropped off for a bit. By the time he awoke, it was nearly sunset.

He locked up the church and made for home, stopping into the strip mall with the liquor store to pick up a fresh box of wine. Then, the heavy cardboard container dangling from one arm, he decided to take another look at the housing development.

Dusk was falling by the time he made it up the hill to the deserted, silent streets. There was something downright spooky in watching the sun set and the streetlights of the uninhabited suburb ghost to life. Barrett had paused at an intersection when the tinkling sound of breaking glass caught his ear. He looked up and scanned the area.

Movement off to his right. Barrett squinted into the shadows between two houses, moving closer. It seemed like something—or someone—was stirring in the darkness there. At first, he thought it might be a stray dog but then the figure rose from the ground and uncurled to full height, revealing it to be a man.

Man, he's big! Barrett thought.

His wonder only deepened when he watched the man reach in through a broken window and remove a huge duffel bag. The bag shattered a few more bits of glass as he hauled it over the sill but he soon pulled it loose and slung it over his shoulder. Then he was turning and hiking across the lawn and deeper into the housing development. Barrett recalled Mick's words.

They call him Kokopeli because anytime anyone's ever caught a glimpse of him, he's always been carrying this huge duffle on his back.

Barrett hid his wine box on the porch of a nearby unit and then set off in pursuit.

Surveillance

BARRETT WAS REMEMBERING.

Usually once in the dead of winter and once again around the summer solstice—someone would break into an empty home and abscond with soap, toilet paper, any spare razors and underwear lying about...

Barrett had mentioned these were odd choices of item for a burglar to rob and Walton had replied...

Not if you're living rough in the woods.

He imagined a man who lives out in the woods, perhaps in a cave or cabin. A man driven mad by loneliness. Someone who had all the normal urges of a man but no outlet. Wouldn't it stand to reason he might crack? Go a little nuts? Do desperate things?

Barrett was familiar with the phenomenon.

Before being sent to Fulton, Barrett had been employed by the Curia as a papal investigator. His work for the Congregation of the Doctrine of the Faith had involved investigating professional misconduct among the clergy. His jab had taken him all over the world—a sort of James Bond with a clerical collar. But touching down in so many ports of call had often held a common theme: that of a hard-working but isolated priest succumbing to his personal demons and surrendering to lustful activities. These activities sometimes involved minors. But not always. So as he followed the shadowy figure across the half-built sprawl of Spirit Ranch, he found himself remembering poor Mrs. Sparrow.

Edgar Sparrow had been the wealthy member of a church congregation in Cape Cod. A fantastically ugly man, he had made a fortune for himself in manufacturing commercial paints. And, like most ugly men with a lot of money, he had used his wealth to purchase the intimacy he could not find naturally in life. At the age of 57, he had arranged to capture a mail-order bride from the Ukraine named Olga, who was all of 22. Attractive, vivacious and well-endowed, she had been a hit in the local Cape Cod social scene and managed to keep Edgar Sparrow good company until his untimely death two years later.

Whereupon, Barrett thought, frowning as the figure ahead turned into a sector of the development littered with construction detritus, *Mrs. Sparrow abruptly vanished.*

Of course, Barrett had known none of this at the time he flew into Cape Cod a year later. He had been sent by the Curia at the request of the local bishop, a man named Hanley, about the behavior of one of his priests. The trip had surprised Barrett. He normally didn't get involved in issues at the diocesan level, and rarely dealt with anyone below the level of archbishop. But when he sat down with Bishop Hanley in his wood paneled office over coffee, he understood the reason for the call.

"The priest at St. Cecilia's in Provincetown is a man

named Donald Duke," Hanley had told him. "Father Duke has been with us for three years now. His first year was satisfactory. Not great, but commendable. The first half of his second year was average, but it's been a downhill slide from there."

"What's going on with him? Is it alcohol?"

"If only it were that simple—that we actually knew what was going on. Unfortunately, we don't." Hanley had shrugged. "Father Duke has become extremely secretive this past year. Almost to the point of being paranoid."

"How so?"

"He fired the parish bookkeeper. Changed the password on all the computers. He's rarely reachable by phone. He seems to have switched his extension to permanent voicemail."

"That *is* odd."

"It gets even odder, Father Barrett. All—I mean *all*—the windows of the rectory have the drapes pulled. He never opens them. Never has visitors. Never goes out anymore. He does services, attends minimal parish duties and then heads straight home. It's gone on long enough that we've become worried. We're hoping you might investigate."

Hanley had arranged for Father Duke to attend a mandatory meeting at his office in another town. This meant an hour's commute either way, allowing Barrett plenty of time to slip inside using the spare key Hanley had on hand. Not technically burglary as the residence was owned by the diocese. If all went well, he would have about three hours to do a little poking around.

Barrett had parked up the street from Duke's residence and waited for the priest to drive away, then waited fifteen minutes and walked up the stairs to the porch and let himself in.

The place had the weird, sterile feel of a freshly cleaned hotel room. Barrett would have ascribed such fastidiousness to the housekeeper, but Father Duke had fired his the year before. All this fresh vacuuming and dusting had been his doing. Barrett found the same barely touched quality in each successive room through which he passed. The hallways, living room, and kitchen were spotless. Even the guest bathroom was unused. Duke's personal quarters were likewise immaculate. The few personal items Barrett found there had the fresh, store-bought look of movie props. It wasn't until Barrett found the door to the basement padlocked that things began to get interesting.

His time on the force had taught him everything he needed to know about picking a lock, and Barrett had made quick work of this one. He had taken the stairs down, only to marvel at what he found.

Duke had created an elaborate fantasy world in his basement: large rubber and plastic bones scattered on a floor of sand, papier-mâché boulders and a low hill inset with a cave's mouth. Inside which had been...

Mrs. Sparrow. Clad in a leopard skin loin cloth and secured by iron chains to the wall. She had greeted Barrett's sudden appearance with a barrage of talk during which she told him everything. How Father Duke had taken to counselling her in the wake of her husband's death, how he had lured her to the rectory to collect the death certificate and then drugged her tea.

"I woke up down here, chained to the wall," she'd said. "He's been coming down here and having his way with me every night. He likes to, uh..." She glanced around at the 'bones' scattered on the floor. "He likes to play caveman."

Barrett chuckled, remembering the flabbergasted expression on Father Duke's face when he returned home to find Barrett waiting with two police officers and an arrest warrant. Barrett had testified at the trial that had ended with Duke sentenced to ten years for rape and kidnapping. Mrs. Sparrow had promptly decamped to Las Vegas, where she met and married a software mogul.

Lot of money in real estate, Barrett thought, glancing around at the moonlit wreckage of the abandoned home sites on this side of Spirit Ranch.

Now the massive figure ahead was slowing. Barrett ducked behind a waist-high wall to observe. The man (Barrett was sure it was a man) was approaching a tin-roofed shed, the kind of place maintenance workers used to store tools. Barrett heard the door squeak and watched the man *(Squatch?)* vanish inside.

Makes sense, Barrett thought. If this was the forest-dweller, then it stood to reason he might search a maintenance shed for useful items. *Guys leave clothes, food, soap in there all the time.*

The man was out again two minutes later. Barrett resumed his surveillance.

The tall figure was heading off-property now. He crossed in front of a framed-out but as-yet incomplete house and stepped over the phoney ranch fence at the far end and started for the trees.

I bet it is him! Barrett thought, picking up speed. He sped across the lawn to the fence, vaulted over it and sprinted for the trees. It was rough going—the ground outside the development was a chaos of splintered rock, discarded timber and felled trees. Barrett lost his footing a few times, stumbling as he reached the treeline. He arrived just in time to see the dim silhouette of the tall man vanish into the shadows of the forest.

Damn!

He bent over, hands on his knees, panting hard. He hadn't run like that in a long time and his cigarette-damaged lungs rebelled with a vengeance. Barrett felt a huge cough gather inside him. He drew a deep breath to dispel it and fell into a jag that ended with him spitting up a lungful of phlegm.

God, I'm out of shape.

He staggered back to the edge of the property. As he was raising a leg to negotiate the fence, a low noise growled in the street beyond. Barrett looked up in time to see Max's Lamborghini flash by, headed into the direction of town. Barrett loped across the yard, back the way he had come. *I'm winded, lost, and hungry,* he thought. It was turning out to be one hell of a day.

He hadn't had a chance to peek into the tin shack so he decided to redress that oversight on the return trip. He staggered through the deserted streets, passing into the construction zone where he remembered the shack being located. It took him a minute or two of casting around to find it, but eventually located its squat shape looming in the shadows. Barrett made for the door and was just reaching for the handle when it occurred to him he didn't have a flashlight. He pulled out removed his lighter and flicked it to life. Then he went in.

The inside of the shack was a mess, a disorganized jumble of clothing, equipment, tools and spare parts. The illumination from the lighter was minimal—a weak globe that pushed back the dark a few feet at best. From the doorway, the scene had been clear. But as Barrett moved into the shack, the globe traveled with him, cutting off a broader view and enclosing him within a sphere of light that illumined only what was directly in front of or on either side of him. He navigated his way between piles of equipment toward a workbench in back. What on Earth had the man come in and removed from this place?

A sound obtruded—a car engine, approaching. Barrett made his way back to the door, pushed it open and listened.

No doubt about it. A car was approaching. Barrett scanned the dark for headlights and found none. Yet he could hear the purr of an engine and the slow roll of tires crunching gravel. And then ..?

Silence. Barrett waited, his eyes closed, for the sound of car doors opening and closing. But no sound came. He decided it must be the sound of Max returning and closed the shack entrance, returning to the workbench, scanning its top in the glow from the lighter.

Nothing. The bench was a scatter of tools and parts. He brushed past a string hanging from above and took a chance that it was connected to a light switch. A quick pull and the shack was bathed in the light from a bare bulb.

Barrett took a careful look around, deciding that if the man he'd been following was the same one who'd broken into his home, he had come in here and left empty-handed. There was nothing even remotely of interest to someone that stole soap and underwear. Barrett was just about to turn out the light when something caught his eye.

There were two cans of black spray paint on the bench. From the scent and the stickiness of their sides, it was obvious they had seen recent use. That's when Barrett remembered his exploration of the unfinished basement, the red hoodie and…

The black pentagram spray-painted on the wall...

A sudden sound alerted him. He switched off the overhead light and listened. Footsteps crunching through gravel, approaching the shack. Barrett ducked down behind a riding mower and waited.

Making New Friends

THE FOOTSTEPS GREW LOUDER. And there was the suggestion of a voice—spoken words? No, *whispered*. Whoever was coming was doing their best to be furtive. Barrett knew instinctively that he was the subject of their search—a knowing that took root and flowered in his gut like a poison plant. He didn't need to reason through it. His present circumstances and the events of the past few days combined to confirm it. Barrett remembered the Glock emblazoned with the Papal Arms that he kept in his kitchen drawer and wished he had it with him.

The steps crunched to a halt outside the door. He heard, rather than saw, it open. Then he saw the swishing beams of flashlights as his pursuers stepped in. The whispers resumed.

"Where?"

"He's in here somewhere!"

"What?"

"There's a light over the workbench. Go switch it on!"

One set of footsteps approached Barrett's position. The workbench was mere feet from him. The man would have to turn his back to reach the cord. Barrett waited until he saw a hand grasping for it in the flashlight's glow before making a move.

He sprang from a crouching position, grabbing for the man and catching hold of some sort of voluminous cloth. *It's one of those damn robes!* In the chaos of a swishing flashlight beam, Barrett could see the dark ceremonial robe, its hood slightly pulled back to reveal the panicked grimace of the wearer. Barrett grappled with him, yanking the robe to unbalance him. He dropped his flashlight onto the workbench. Barrett grabbed it up, swung hard and bashed the guy across the teeth with it. Glass shattered and the man's abortive scream died in a mumble as he spat out blood and shattered glass. Before he could recover, Barrett smashed the handle of the flashlight, heavy with batteries, against the man's skull, driving him into unconsciousness.

The other man leapt, but Barrett was ready for him. He kicked out hard, the heel of his shoe connecting with the man's lower belly. He sought to bring his flashlight to bear, trying to blind Barrett, but to no avail. He was already down on one knee. Barrett aimed a kick at his face, looking for the knockout. But he was off center. His heel connected with the man's shoulder, driving him backwards against the door. Before Barrett could land on top of him, he had twisted to his feet, battered his way through the door and was fleeing up the path at top speed.

Barrett stood panting heavily for a few moments before switching on the workbench light.

The Satanist lay in a tangled heap on the ground. Barrett rolled him over, checked for a pulse, pushed open an eyelid. The guy was still breathing, but out like a light. He would come to sooner or later.

Barrett smiled coldly.

He had plans for this son-of-a-bitch.

———

THE ROBED MAN STIRRED. He mumbled and squirmed, smacking his lips. With a squint and hard blink, he opened his eyes.

Barrett sat before him in a kitchen chair, a glass of wine in one hand and the box on the table beside him. He watched coldly as the robed man looked around the rectory kitchen before seeing Barrett and starting. It was only when he tried to stand and flee that he noticed he was tied to the chair.

"Oh, don't worry," Barrett said conversationally, refilling his glass. "I probably won't actually *kill* you. But, ah, once I'm done? You'll wish I had."

Barrett rose, stepped forward and jerked the hood back from the man's head. He was a balding, forty-something with watery eyes, jowls and a weak chin. To Barrett's eyes, he looked like the sort of man who flew a desk. *Probably a chartered accountant or software designer,* he thought before returning to his chair.

"There. Much better!" Barrett resumed drinking. "Now I can see your bright, shiny face. No secrets between us, eh? We're all friends here."

A look of sheer terror seized the robed man's face. Eyes wide and teeth gritted, he began shaking his head furiously back and forth. Trying to clear it? Or convince himself that what he was seeing wasn't real? Barrett wasn't sure. He chuckled, putting down his wine and walking to the stove.

"You know, when I was a kid, we used to do this

thing called 'hot knives.'" Barrett switched on an element, opened a side drawer and reached inside. "It was a good way to do hashish without the inconvenience of buying pipes, rolling papers, all that garbage. See, what you did was you stuck a couple of knives into the stove element, heated them up and then placed a ball of hash on one knife before pressing it down with the other. It super-heated the hash to ash and you sucked down the smoke through a toilet paper tube. Ah! The good old days…"

Barrett withdrew his hand, holding a clutch of forks and knives.

"I'm feeling mighty nostalgic right now." He began inserting cutlery into the prongs of the warming element. "Doing this brings me right back to high school. Me and Chris McKenna and Billy Wright, heating knives and breaking sticky little blocks of hash into little balls… Man, those were good times."

He turned from the stove and looked around theatrically.

"But hey! I don't have any hashish! What a bummer. I forgot all about that. You wouldn't happen to have any, would you?"

The man made a noise like a cow trying to moo through clenched teeth.

"Didn't think so. You don't look like the type." Barrett toasted him. "Never mind. We have plenty of wine. Oops! Perhaps I should say… *I* have plenty of wine. You don't get any. Sorry! But that's what happens when you kidnap and rough up a priest. Ten Hail Marys and *no wine for you* until I see some attitude adjust-ment!" He chuckled, swallowed his drink, and put down his glass.

The robed man said nothing.

"So tell me," Barrett said casually, going to the stove. "What's your name, pal?"

The man remained silent.

"Okay." Barrett grabbed a heated fork from the stove element. "I suppose a little encouragement is in order…"

Barrett advanced, holding the fork out before him like a dagger level with the man's left eyeball. The Satanist held his composure for all of ten seconds before renewing his struggle against the ropes. But Barrett had tied him tightly to the seat. His frantic squirms managed to jar the chair an inch or so to the left. But that was all.

Barrett placed a hand on his shoulder, pushing the fork's superheated tines toward his eye.

"Okay! Okay! Okay!" The man trembled as he stared at the approaching prongs. "My name is Brian, okay? Brian Edwards!"

"Brian…*Edwards*. There!" Barrett patted the shoulder and turned away. "See how easy that was? Nice to meet you, Brian." Barrett threw the heated fork into the partially filled sink, where it sank with a hiss. "I'm guessing you must have been there the other night. In the library. With, ah, Frater Nox?"

Edwards looked dumbstruck. "How do you…"

"How do I know his super-duper secret ceremonial name?" Barrett lifted and swallowed down his wine before refilling it. "That's the thing, Bri. We priests know *all sorts of things* that you civilians don't. For example, that the Black Star Temple has deep pockets. *Very* deep. Like, *so* deep that they can afford to loan people money."

Edwards' lips trembled.

"People like Arnold McLellan. Who, as you know, doesn't usually have problems borrowing money. But if he happens to suddenly need ten million bucks…"

Edwards' eyes shot wide.

"There. See? I figured you knew about it. What are you? Temple bookkeeper? Financial advisor? Something like that?"

"S—something. Like. That."

"Mm. Let's find out what else you know." Barrett dragged a heated steak knife from the element and held up the point for Edwards to see. "Know what I love about these? Is the way they can shear apart meat and gristle. Even if wedged into a tiny little space. Like, say, between a fingernail and the flesh beneath it…"

"*Nnnnnnoooooo!*"

"Oh, *yes!*" Barrett smacked his thigh. "Amazing invention, the steak knife! Right up there with the musket, the microwave, the personal computer! Let's hear it for the creative intellect of Man!" Barrett seized up more wine, killed a whole glass with one swallow, and reset his footing as dizziness swam in his head. *Better take it easy,* he warned himself.

Edwards swallowed. "I'll tell you anything you want to know. Anything at all."

"Does the Black Star Temple have a glee club?"

"A—what? Um, no. No glee club."

"Of course not! You Satanists are a glum bunch of fuckers, aren't you? I betchya got no hymns, either. Huh? Nothing jaunty like *Amazing Grace* or *Nearer My God to Thee*?" Barrett grabbed the man's wrist. Edwards immediately balled it into a fist. So Barrett inserted the hot knife in the crack between fingers and palm and pushed.

Edwards loosed the most godawful shriek Barrett had ever heard and immediately opened his hand, unclutching his burned and bloody fingers and allowing the knife to clatter to the linoleum. Barrett seized it up and tossed it into the dishwater. *Hisssss.* Then he went back to the stove.

"Tell me about the kids, Edwards."

"Kids?"

"Yes! The kids! The goddam kids that are going missing around here! You Satanic bastards are behind it, aren't you?"

Edwards gaped, his expression blank.

"Oh, now!" Barrett grinned. "Such theatrics! I'm thinking you must have drama experience. Because that look of absolute ignorance is just…" He brought three fingers to his mouth and gave a chef's kiss. *"Magnifique!* Truly believable. Now." Barrett plucked a butter knife from the element. "Tell me. About. The kids."

Edwards opened his mouth and seemed about to speak when his breath hitched on something. A burp? A bunch of phlegm? Barrett couldn't tell. All he knew was that Edwards' face was reddening and he was flopping around on the chair now, quivering and drooling. His eyes, when they rolled Barrett's way, were watery and unfocused.

He's having a damn seizure! Barrett plucked the steak knife from the sink and set to attacking Edwards' bonds —no easy task given how much the man was writhing around. But within a minute he had them loose and was lowering Edwards to the floor, turning him into the recovery position to let his mouth drain. A pool of spit formed on the floor below his chin.

Barrett reached for the First Aid kit under the sink. He wasn't sure if Edwards' sudden convulsions were due to epilepsy or a seizure, both having a stout roll of bandage to jam between the guy's teeth seemed like a good idea. He was rooting in the kit when Edwards suddenly sprang to his feet.

"Hey!" Barrett dropped the kit. "Wait just a—"

Then Edwards was sprinting down the hallway to the

front door, robes flapping behind him. Barrett managed to catch hold of them and yank, slowing the man for a second. But then Edwards turned, pulled his robe free, and gained the front door.

"You're crazy!" he screamed at Barrett, twisting the knob and pulling. He launched himself onto the porch, down the steps, and into the street. Barrett watched him dash off into the night, robe askew, heels pounding the pavement as he grew smaller and smaller before finally disappearing into the shadows.

"Son-of-a-bitch," Barrett sighed.

He closed and locked the door, then returned to the kitchen. He switched off the element, gathered up the bits of rope and cleaned Edwards' blood and spit from the linoleum to sit down and finish his drink.

Update

"...JUST discovered the spray paint cans when all of a sudden, *WHAM!* In come these two guys wearing robes —same kind the guys who kidnapped me wore. They attacked me."

Lewis, standing in the shadowed half-light of the ICU room, blinked in surprise. "They attacked you, padre? Really?"

"Yep." Barrett fetched a heavy sigh, using the time to frame his story carefully. He didn't want there to be any holes. "Just came at me, fists swinging. I took out the one guy right away. Cold cocked him with his own flashlight. The other guy put up more of a fight. I managed to subdue him and force him to answer some questions."

"So—wait a minute." Lewis was pulling out his notebook and pen. "You're figuring these guys are connected to the group that kidnapped and threatened you, the 'Black Star Temple.' The ones that warned you to stay away from the housing development?"

"Right. And I got a name. Brian Edwards."

"Interesting, Okay." Lewis wrote that down. "I'll run

him and see if he's in AIPIC. Meanwhile, what happened with Edwards?"

"He managed to break free and escape before I could call you." Barrett congratulated himself on painting a picture that left him more or less blameless. "But there's more. I have reason to believe this temple may be tied to McLellan and his investment in Spirit Ranch. Edwards brought his name up."

"In what context?"

"Something to the effect that McLellan was in their bad books." Barrett shrugged. "I intended to follow up and get more but by then he had broken free and fled." He left it at that, not yet willing to disclose his visit with McLellan and Frater Nox. Barrett considered it his last pastoral visit to the man and so kept it confidential.

Old habits die hard, Barrett reminded himself. *And not just in monasteries.*

"I looked into the Black Star Temple," Lewis told him. "Folks down in Victoria have an extensive database on occult crime. There's a ton of it down there. All manner of temples, groves, churches and the like… Some with damned exotic names. But nothing about this Black Star organization. Sounds like they keep a low profile, even among the occult community."

"Makes sense," Barrett said. "If they're involved in dark, infernal matters, they wouldn't exactly be welcome among a community that's trying hard to rehabilitate its image as your 'friendly pagans next door.'"

"Roger that."

A knock at the open door. They turned to see Walton enter the empty ward and join them standing over Jason Joe's bed. The boy was still unconscious.

"How's our guy?" Walton asked, nodding to Jason Joe.

"We're about to get an update, here." Lewis glanced toward the charge nurse's desk. She had left to consult with the doctor. "You find anything?"

"Yeah." Walton produced his own notebook and flipped through a few pages before settling on one. "Had a chat with a Conservation colleague in Nanaimo. He's well connected with folks in the RCMP detachment down there. There has definitely been an uptick in activity among the Vietnamese gangs, one in particular." Walton frowned at his notes. "Can't pronounce their name but my friend says the Mounties are bird-dogging them something awful. Apparently, they suspect a high volume of human traffic is moving through the port. All they have now are some tips and a few blurry photographs, but they're working the case hard."

The nurse entered just as Walton was finishing up. Lewis favored her with a smile.

"How is he?" he asked.

"Well, as you can see…" The nurse flipped some pages on her clipboard. "Still unconscious. His vitals are stable, which is encouraging. At some point he's going to wake up. We're pretty confident about that." She squinted at a print-out. "X-rays and CAT scans came back fine. So far as we can tell, no internal injuries of note. Um, one thing. It's kind of a small detail, but I know for police work that any information is useful. So." She dropped her finger to the page. "Lab work came back with something interesting. Blood work suggests that, at some point in the recent past, Jason here inhaled a fair amount of a chemical we've identified as concrete sealant."

Lewis raised his eyebrows. "That *is* significant."

"Thought so." The nurse placed the clipboard on the bedside table and pulled the blanket up around the sleeping boy. "That's all we've got for you today, sergeant. Let's leave the boy to rest quietly."

"Of course." Lewis nodded to her and led the other two out of the room. When they paused in the hallway, he turned to Barrett. "Keep digging, father. But be careful."

Barrett smiled. "I will."

"Hey, padre," said Walton. "How's your dog?"

"He's not my dog," mumbled Barrett. And was surprised at the pang of guilt he felt for abandoning Asshole. He resolved to check in on Scooter.

––––––

HE DIDN'T GET AROUND to it until later in the afternoon. It was late enough in the day that the sun was slanting toward the western horizon when Barrett marched around to the parking lot behind the church and knocked on the door of the venerable RV parked there. Footsteps sounded inside and the unit shook as Scooter answered.

"Heya, father!" The caretaker flashed a gap-toothed grin from beneath the brim of his weathered ballcap. "Was just about to pop open a beer. Care for one?"

"Sure." Barrett followed Scooter into the trailer. The tidy, darkened interior of the RV served as Scooter's home and "man cave." With the curtains drawn and John Coltrane on the sound system, it was more like a gentleman's club than a home. Barrett took a seat on the padded bench in the nook behind the kitchen table and looked around. "Where's As– I mean, the dog?"

Scooter turned from the fridge, two cans of beer in hand. He gave a brief, shrill whistle and Asshole came bounding out of the bedroom.

"There he is!" enthused Scooter. He set one can down in front of Barrett and popped the other, bending to scratch the mutt behind the ears. "Howza boy? Eh? Howza good boy?" As Barrett watched, Scooter leaned over and poured a quantity of beer into a bowl on the floor. Asshole eagerly lumbered over and began snuffling it up.

"You're corrupting him," Barrett noted, popping his can and taking a sip of Lucky.

"Winston? Nah." Scooter grinned as he took a seat. "He's a beer drinking fool, is my Winston!"

"*My* Winston?" Barrett was surprised to feel a pang inside. "I see you've named him…"

"Yeah. Winston. After Churchill. Dog kinda' resembles him, don't you think?"

"I dunno." Barrett frowned. "Stick a bowler hat on his head and a stogie in his mouth and I'll tell you." He took a sip. "Listen, Scooter. I wanted to ask you something. Has to do with occult activity around Fulton."

"Occult?" Scooter frowned, plainly disliking the topic. "Thank God, we've been spared much of that crap…"

"How do you mean?"

"You just moved to the island this year, didn't you?" Scooter was studying him.

"Yeah." Barrett burped. "In October. When I took over the parish."

"So, you don't know." Scooter stared into the middle distance, looking grim. "This island has a history of that kind of thing. And I'm not talking about the Natives and their superstitions, here. I'm talking about white folks and their drawing-room Satanism. Don't look surprised, father! Did you know that Victoria has the highest concentration of witches of any city in North America?"

"No. I didn't." Barrett felt suddenly queasy.

"Oh, yeah!" Scooter took a long swallow of beer and fisted his hand on the table. "Those damn richies, father. Having more money than Croesus ain't enough for them. They like to believe they can control reality, to boot. Curses and spells, hocus-pocus and other nonsense. Very fashionable among the upper crust, donchya know. We've been lucky around here. And I give credit to the Indians."

"You mean, the tribe?"

"Yup." Scooter nodded emphatically. "A lot of 'em are Christian. And the ones that aren't practice their old ways, which are gentle, nature-spirit beliefs. Their kind don't sort with sorcerers and witches and the like. Why, one summer about five years back a Native man came into town, claiming he was a shaman and could speak to the dead. You shoulda seen how fast the Chief and his cronies ran his sorry ass outta town. Guy barely escaped with the clothes on his back!" He wheezed laughter. "It doesn't pay to mess with the tribe. Especially where spiritual matters are concerned. So, no. Not much occult crap going on hereabouts, father."

"That's good to know. Thanks." Barrett drained his beer and stood. "Thanks for the drink. I'll take the dog back…"

"Er, father." Scooter looked embarrassed. "Are you still looking for a home for Winston? Because, truth be told… I'm kinda' getting attached to the little fellow…"

Barrett held up his hands. "He's yours," he said with relief.

THE EVENING WAS MOVING toward dusk as he crossed the parking lot and stopped into the church. He checked the phone messages, glanced through the mail Scooter had left in his inbox and inspected his vestments and sacraments for Sunday's service. Then he reset the burglar alarm and let himself out to resume the walk home.

Scooter's words rattled him. He had had no idea there was so much occult activity on the island. But it made a weird sort of sense. The wealthy were heavily represented here, both legacy money from the timber and fishing industry as well as the nouveau riche that had fled here to their condos and hobby farms to escape the rat race on the mainland. Barrett thought it was entirely possible some of the occult groups traced their lineage back to the late 19th Century, a time when spiritualism, table-tapping and séances had gripped the western imagination.

The roots of this go deep, he thought. *No telling how deep.*

He didn't hear the sound of the sirens until he was almost home. He stopped and listened. Fulton, despite its crime problem, was rarely a town where you heard sirens. Lewis had told him he felt they were often inappropriate for the kinds of calls they received. *Sirens,* he'd told Barrett, *are big city sound effects designed to establish presence and produce shock.* As an ex-cop, Barrett had to agree. He couldn't recall ever having heard them here before.

And yet now they were blaring loud as Hades and creeping closer. Barrett was looking up the street when Lewis' car swept around the corner, lights and sirens going like the very bells of Hell itself, Walton's Conservation Service truck close behind. Lewis braked to a halt beside Barrett, killed the siren and rolled down the window.

"We got trouble, padre!"

"What's up?" Barrett stepped to the window and bent.

"Just had a call. All hell has broken loose at Spirit Ranch Estates. Walton and I could use a hand."

"Sure thing." Barrett yanked open the passenger door and clipped himself into the seat. Lewis flicked the siren back on and floored the car. "What's going on?" Barrett asked, the siren muffled by the car's sound-proofed interior.

"Take a look." Lewis nodded through the window.

Barrett did. A plume of smoke was climbing skyward from the development. "What the hell…"

"Got a call from Mabel Rigby. She was out walking her dog. Said she saw a big group of Indians heading up the hill. She said they looked mad as hell."

"They're attacking the estate?"

"Apparently so. Smashing things up. Setting buildings on fire. The natives are restless."

"Good lord," muttered Barrett.

"In the middle of everything else, this is all I need," muttered Lewis. He slowed as he approached the road to the estate and turned. Barrett saw flames rising to the sky.

Rampage

LEWIS STEERED the Crown Vic into Spirit Ranch, lights and sirens wailing, Walton close behind him in the Conservation truck. They made for the flames.

"There!" Barrett pointed out the windshield. "Look!"

A jumble of battered cars and haphazardly parked pick-ups jammed the intersection ahead. Lewis brought the patrol car to a stop and cursed. "What the hell's going on?" he muttered, slamming the Crown Vic into park and bailing out, Barrett and Walton right behind him.

Barrett followed Lewis into the intersection. He counted ten vehicles, plus five more parked by the curb. A crowd of about thirty town locals was gathering in the street. A number of them carried baseball bats and tire irons. These weren't the Chief's people, Barrett realized. This crowd was comprised of small shop owners, day laborers, and blue-collar types. A man in a red and white checkered jacket was addressing them.

"...bad enough that the government lets them blockade railways and roads! Now they're burning down houses! When the fuck are the cops gonna *do* something? I say we—"

"Okay, that's *enough!*" Lewis waded into the crowd, pushing people back. "What the hell is going on here?"

"We could ask you the same thing, Lewis!" bellowed a man from the crowd. "Goddam Indians are burning the place down! And where the hell are you?"

"*I* am right here!" Lewis spread his legs and gripped his gun belt. "Law and order in this town is kept by right of the Crown! Not some goddam mob! Fire Department's on its way! You folks need to clear your vehicles out of the road to give them access! And then *go the hell home* before I start making arrests!"

The assembled men listened but didn't seem inclined to comply. Barrett shifted nervously from foot to foot. There were just the three of them against a mob that had them outnumbered ten to one. When Lewis was finished, they began crowding in closer. They were done listening.

"Where the hell were you when this started?" demanded the man in the checkered jacket. "It shouldn't be us coming up here to deal with it!"

"You're *right!*" Lewis shot back. "It shouldn't be you! Now go home, dammit!"

Some of the men in the crowd were muttering angrily, squaring their shoulders and adjusting their grips on their weapons. Barrett pushed through the crowd until he stood beside Lewis.

"Every moment we stand here arguing is another moment something can go up in flames!" he cried. "Sergeant Lewis, Officer Walton and I are here and *we* will deal with the tribe! Please! We don't want anyone getting hurt!"

"Only ones gonna' get hurt are them Natives!"

snarled a voice from the crowd. Raucous laughter and cheers rose in response. Walton had begun pushing his way through the mob toward Lewis.

"Padre." Lewis had gripped Barrett's arm and hissed in his ear. "Walton and I will handle this. Go find the Chief and get him to cease and desist. We'll deal with these guys."

Barrett nodded and turned, crossing the lawn of a half-built house toward the fire as the shouts and noise of the crowd faded behind him. A fever of frenzy built inside him as he pushed speed into his legs, lungs burning, head fogged from drink (or maybe lack thereof). But he didn't care. He had to find the Chief and whoever was with him and put a stop to this before things got even worse.

He reached the edge of the lawn, crossed between two finished houses, and skidded to a stop on the curb. He had gone up a block and arrived on the next street. He scanned around. *There!* He saw a cluster of folks half-a-block up, their backs to him. As Barrett approached, he noted two women, one in a Canucks hoodie and the other wrapped in a blanket, filming something with her cell phone. A trio of kids clustered around their knees.

"Hi! Hey there!" Barrett waved. "Where's the Chief?"

The woman in the blanket turned, resentment hardening in her wide, dark eyes. "What you want, father?" she snarled. "You come here because you think you can *help* us? How much help were you when they were stealing our kids and putting them in residential schools?"

Barrett put up his hands. "Look. I'm sorry. I really am. About the things that happened. But right now, I need to talk to the Chief. You guys are in real danger."

"Why?" The woman in the hoodie had turned and joined the conversation. "*We're* in danger? Why? Is there a bunch of Mounties down there ready to come rough us up?"

"The only Mountie down there is Gavin Lewis and he's doing everything he can to make sure this thing ends without loss of life."

"Loss of life?" Blanket Woman laughed. "That a threat, father?"

Barrett's frustration built. "There's a mob of angry townspeople down there with baseball bats! They've come to crack skulls!"

"Let 'em come!" Hoodie Woman was defiant. "You think you can scare us?"

"I don't want to scare anybody." Barrett felt suddenly very tired. "I just want to make sure nobody gets hurt."

Something in his tone of voice, or his facial expression perhaps, caused the women to relent. They exchanged a glance.

"He's down that way," Blanket Woman said finally, pointing up the street.

"Thank you." Barrett sprinted off in that direction.

The flames were closer now, clawing the sky in gouts of black smoke. *There!* Barrett paused in the intersection. A half-finished unit engulfed in flames backlit the scene. He saw flickering shadows moving around its base. The silhouette of a man holding a gas can, his back to Barrett, raised his left arm and made a fist.

"Hey!" Barrett yelled, waving. "Hey! Where's the Chief?"

The man with the gas can turned, saw Barrett, and lumbered off, ignoring the question.

Barrett raced toward the fire, soon finding himself

adrift amidst a galaxy of milling shadows. Men and women moved around the burning frames and buildings. Some carried gas cans, others waved torches. A weird joy infused them—a hilarity mixed with rage that swirled like the stench of gasoline filling the air.

God in heaven, Barrett thought. He appreciated their outrage, their sense of betrayal that had fermented into this violence. But it had to stop before things truly got out of hand. He whirled, looking from place to place until he saw a group of people around a man in shorts and a baseball cap. *The Chief!* Barrett sprinted over.

"Chief!" Barrett waved his hands. "Chief, please! May I speak with you?"

The Chief and the group around him turned. Barrett felt their eyes upon him, weighing, judging, measuring. The Chief's ordinarily friendly face was a stone mask. Barrett felt a wave of unease wash over him. He knew the Chief to be a reasonable man—a good man who would never countenance violence…

But even good men can be pushed too far.

"Father." The Chief's voice suggested a strong effort to control his temper. "You should not be here. This is our business—Indian business. Your church has no place with us."

"Black coat!" spat one young man, waggling the gas can in his fist. "Get outta here!"

The cry was taken up by the assembled Natives, one or two even breaking ranks to advance menacingly on Barrett.

"Please!" He held up his hands. "You don't understand! A mob is coming! Lewis is trying to hold them off but they're coming here to do you harm!"

"Then let them come!" The Chief's voice boomed,

stilling those of the others around him who fell silent with eerie precision. His next words were echoed only by the sound of crackling flames. "My people have endured two centuries of oppression! From the settlers to the church to the politicians! Now the financiers and property developers have jumped on the band wagon to keep us down! No more! No more!"

Barrett's heart broke as he listened. Of *course* the Chief was right. The trail of Confederation was littered with the broken bodies and souls of First Nations people. But Barrett would be damned if he would allow any more bodies to be added tonight.

"You're in *danger!* The townspeople are coming!" Barrett addressed them all. "Some are armed! Lewis is trying to hold them off…"

"Here they come!" cried Blanket Woman, who had joined the group around the Chief. Barrett turned.

Like a rolling wave, the crowd of thirty or so townspeople was advancing up the street. Their footsteps, their muttered voices radiated menace. The energy of mob violence swirled around them.

"Get stones," ordered the Chief. "You young men, form a line here! Women and kids, get back behind them!"

"Chief." Barrett gripped the old man's arm. "Don't do this!"

"Don't tell us what to do, father." The Chief's gaze, half-lidded and resolute, settled on Barrett, who released the man's arm.

What the hell do I do now?

Barrett knew.

He drew a deep breath, remembering the police and firefighters who rushed into the Twin Towers on 9/11.

When they went to work that morning, they'd had no idea what they would be asked to do that day. Those men had sworn an oath to their communities and their Constitution. Barrett's oath was to a much higher authority.

Who does the hard jobs? Barrett gritted his teeth. *He who can.*

He turned and ran toward the mob of approaching townsmen. When he was halfway between them and the Chief's people, he raised his hand.

"STOP!" His voice boomed. "In the name of human decency! In the name of *God!* I demand that you stop and lay down your arms!"

The mob slowed. A few of the men in the front ranks exchanged glances. Barrett didn't like the way they were smiling.

"You best get out of our way, father!" cried the man in the checkered jacket. "Your collar won't save you now!"

"My *collar?*" Barrett gripped it with his hand and ripped it off, holding it out to them. "You want a collar, here it is! You want to *kill* somebody? Kill me! *But leave these people alone, for God's sake!"*

The mob resumed its advance, all eyes boring into Barrett as he stood there. Barrett dropped his collar and began to pray.

Heavenly father, if my body can slow them down even for a few seconds...

He was ready.

And then suddenly the shriek of an engine and the squeal of brakes sounded behind him. He spun. Lewis had rolled up in his Crown Vic, with Walton right behind him in the Conservation truck. They screeched to a halt between the Natives and the advancing crowd.

Both men leapt out. Walton held his shotgun in hand and Lewis cradled a C8 automatic rifle. He moved up in front of Barrett and addressed the advancing townspeople.

"THIS ENDS NOW!" he bellowed. *"By order of the Crown, you will disperse and return to your homes immediately or we will employ lethal force! This is your first and final warning!"*

Lewis cocked the rifle, threw it to his shoulder, and sighted along the barrel at the townsmen.

"Now git!" he ordered.

The mob paused, the leaders suddenly unsure. A voice rose from the back of the crowd.

"He won't shoot!" a man cried. "Come on! Let's finish this!"

Lewis raised the rifle and fired a round into the air above the crowd's head.

"I can switch this thing to full auto!" he warned. "I'll shred you bastards like a goddam wood chipper! You want to take that chance?"

It was enough to deter them. A few at the rear of the crowd began drifting away. Barrett turned to see the Chief close behind him, disbelief in his eyes.

"I can't believe it," muttered the Chief. "I can't believe Lewis would do that for us…"

"What? You think he doesn't care about you? You think *we* don't care about you?"

Walton and Lewis were advancing on the crowd now, which was thinning fast. Men turned and went back the way they came. A few defiant stragglers yelled and threw the finger, but even they were backpedalling. Barrett breathed a sigh of relief. A massacre had been averted.

That's when he caught sight of a familiar shape

loping across the lawn between two houses across the street. The tall man with the duffel bag.

Squatch!

With one last look to make sure the mob situation was now under control, Barrett fixed his eyes on the man's silhouette and took off after him.

Informant

I'M NOT LETTING *him get away this time.*

Barrett's senses were on heightened alert. He forgot about the pain and fatigue, the aches in his body and mind. Bent at the waist and crouched forward, he moved fast, the adrenalin coursing through his veins, eyes and mind pulsing with energy. He was on a man hunt, and it remained every bit the rush it had been since his days in the Toronto PD.

Squatch vanished into the backyard of a completed house. Barrett poured on the speed, rounding the corner in time to see him climbing the fence into the yard of the house behind it. Barrett moved into the shadow of the foliage at the yard's edge, using it for cover as he approached the fence. Squatch had crossed the next yard and was making for the street beyond. Barrett waited until he had crossed into the shadow of the house before going after him.

He stepped over the fence and resumed his crouching run, formulating a plan to capture the man. So far, Squatch had given no indication of knowing he was being stalked. *And he's weighed down by that bag,* Barrett thought. The element of surprise was on his side. *I'll jump him from behind,* he thought, flattening himself against the house and peering around the corner. No sign of Squatch.

Damn, he's fast! Barrett took the corner, sprinting for the front yard. He was almost there when something heavy flattened him.

Barrett went face-down into the lawn, the breath blown out of him. Squatch had been lying in wait. Now Barrett was underneath him, struggling to escape. *Hell, struggling to BREATHE!* The man was massive, his weight pressing down like the proverbial ton of bricks. No matter how hard he struggled, Barrett could gain no purchase. He grunted and squirmed like a flattened frog.

"Stop wiggling!" Squatch grunted. "Stupid priest!"

Barrett complied. Because he wasn't getting anywhere and besides, he was having trouble breathing. He lay still, the smell of dirt and lawn filling his sinuses.

"I'm gonna get up, father. But don't run. Because I wanna show you something."

Show me something? Barrett's surprise was massive but under the circumstances, he could only express it by blinking. Moments later, the weight was lifted from his back as Squatch rose. Barrett put his hands on the grass and groaned as he pushed himself upright. He stood shakily and turned to Squatch.

He was indeed a massive man. More than six feet tall, broad shouldered and bearded, he resembled a mountain man from the old west. The clothing he wore —a Mackinaw jacket, stout slacks, boots, and a toque— was sturdy but patched. Barrett saw curiosity on the man's face and a fierce intelligence gleaming in the eyes.

"You shouldna followed me, father. I just wanna be

left alone!" His voice was guttural, phlegmy. "But I guess it's good that you did. Because I been trying to tell you."

"Huh?" Barrett finally caught his breath. He couldn't believe what he was hearing. "What do you mean you've been 'trying to tell me'?"

"When I broke into your house." Squatch's eyes narrowed. "You think I'd break into a priest's house? Maybe when I was younger, but not these days. No way. I don't sort with church people or any of that organized religious bullshit, but I respect priests. Didn't used to but I do now. I broke into your house to send a message."

"What message?"

"Same one I was trying to send when I left that red hoodie in the basement of the house. I saw you go explore that one place with Sergeant Lewis. Figured you'd find it sooner or later and catch on."

"Wait. *You* left the—"

"Yeah, I left the hoodie." Squatch adjusted the fit of the huge duffel over his shoulder. "I didn't kidnap the kid who was wearing it. But I know where he is."

"You...*what?*"

"I know where *they* are."

With that, the giant turned his back on Barrett and continued on course through the development. The sounds of the panic faded behind him, replaced by the distant wail of approaching fire engines.

Squatch approached a finished house now, walking with real purpose, Barrett hurrying to catch up with him. The giant paused at the front door.

"This is where he's been keeping them," Squatch said, touching the door. "I never break into these places. No soap or toilet paper, right? But this one I went into. Didn't have to break a window. He left the sliding glass door unlocked after his last visit." He stared at Barrett. "They're in here."

"Who's in there?"

"The missing kids."

"And who did you see putting them there?"

"You'll figure it out." Squatch sighed and stared longing across the development toward the forest beyond. "Father, I just want to get the hell out of here and go back home. I got nothing to do with this. And I don't even want to get involved. But it ain't right. It just isn't."

Squatch began lumbering toward the trees.

"Wait!" Barrett cried. When the giant turned, he implored him. "At least give me a hint!"

Squatch smiled. "He's got a helluva nice car for a groundskeeper, doesn't he?"

That was all he said. But it was enough. Realization dawned on Barrett as he watched the man disappear into the trees. Then Barrett whirled, raised a leg and kicked open the door.

———

A SENSE of wrongness hit him right away. He knew it. He'd sensed it before entering the homes of victims, both those he'd encountered as a cop and the ones he'd met as a priest. It was as if victimhood itself had a stench, and Barrett supposed it very possibly did. It was the stench of betrayed trust, confusion and burned dreams. And he felt it here in the entry hall of this model home. No furniture, but...

Jackets. For some reason there were jackets hung on the open rack in the nook behind the entryway. *And footwear on the floor...* Barrett counted three pairs of shoes. That's when a chill seized him.

All kid's sizes.

His priest's instinct made him want to cry out hello, is there anyone there? But the cop inside him stepped forward and cupped a hand over Barrett's mouth. *What if the traffickers are here?* he thought. And so proceeded with caution.

A black shirt, black pants, black shoes... Traditional priestly garb was perfect for ninja work. Barrett had discovered this during his last investigation for Lewis, a sordid affair involving missing persons, assault, and theft of mortal remains. His clothing had allowed him to narrowly evade notice of a biker gang he happened to be spying on. As he hoped it might save him now, if necessary.

He crept along the short hallway to what was obviously meant to be the kitchen. Recesses built for stoves and refrigerators yawned empty, filled only with shadows. A low half-wall gave out onto what was meant to be a family room. A fireplace had been installed...

Barrett stopped dead. There, scattered on the carpet before the hearth, was a collection of crushed beer cans and empty bottles, empty packages of pretzels and potato chips and packets of cigarettes. Ashes and butts littered the floor of the fireplace.

But there's no sign of anyone.

A short hallway from the family room led to a laundry room (more empty recesses) and two back bedrooms. All were empty. It was only upon his return that Barrett noticed the door to the basement near the entry hall.

Missed it on the way by, he thought, grasping the handle. To his surprise, there were bulbs dangling from the ceiling and a pull-cord at the head of the stairs. He tugged it and blinked as he walked down at a flight of wooden steps descending into the basement. He took the steps down quickly, minimizing the chance of ambush if anyone lay in wait. No one did. No one who could do him any harm, at any rate.

He reached the bottom of the steps and froze.

Across the room from him were four children, two girls and two boys. All were wearing stout leather dog collars, each of which was chained to a large block of concrete set into the floor.

Barrett bit back his horror, closed his eyes, and tried hard not to scream.

Then he was moving toward them, hands raised. "It's okay, it's okay." He barely managed to get these words out between gasps. He approached one kid, reaching for the collar so he could examine it when the kid recoiled in obvious terror. Barrett smiled and tried again. "It's okay…I'm a priest. I'm not going to hurt you."

"He doesn't understand you," said one of the girls. She appeared to be Chinese. "He only speaks Dutch."

"How long have you been here?" Barrett asked. Each of the collars was inset with an iron ring to which each chain was attached.

"We came at different times. The latest to come is her." The Chinese girl turned and pointed to Sabrina. Then she picked up a torn collar still attached to its own chain although its captive had fled. "There was a Native boy with us…"

"Jason Joe."

"Yeah." The Chinese girl dropped the collar. "That's him. He managed somehow to get out."

"Okay." Barrett held up a hand. "Stand by."

He dragged out his cellphone, hit the speed dial

button and called Lewis, who answered on the second ring.

"This better be good, padre. My hands are kinda' full just now."

"I have a house full of children who are chained in dog collars in the basement. Sabrina's here, along with three others."

"Jesus! Hang on." Then Lewis was crying out to a group of people who Barrett assumed was the assembled tribesmen. "Okay! We're coming! Where are you?"

"I'll be standing at the door. It's two streets up from where you guys are. We're going to need firemen to cut some chains. And get Rusty and that other paramedic up here."

"Yep. Yep. On it." Lewis hung up.

Barrett folded and put away his phone, then turned back to the girl.

"The man who did this to you." Barrett spoke slowly and clearly. "A guy about thirty? In a ballcap and work shirt?"

The Chinese girl nodded. "And a real loud car," she said. "He took Sabrina's shoes for some reason. I don't know why."

"Thanks." Barrett smiled. "Sit tight. The police will be here any second."

Barrett turned and took the stairs two at a time back to the ground floor and moved to the entry hall where the broken front door was dangling on its hinges. He moved outside to stand on the stoop. He didn't have to wait long. Within two minutes, a gaggle of voices rose, preceding the crowd of Natives led by Lewis, Walton, and the Chief. The latter was the first to reach Barrett.

"They're downstairs," Barrett told him. "Sabrina's there, Chief."

"Thank goodness," breathed the Chief. Then he turned and snapped a few words in his language and three of the older women in the group came to him immediately. They proceeded downstairs as a group, followed by Lewis. Walton lingered for a moment with Barrett outside the front door, cradling the shotgun which had gone thankfully unused that night.

"You go on in, Adam." Barrett smiled. "I'll watch the door."

"Thanks." Walton clapped his shoulder. "Gavin will want to talk to you anyway. Get a statement."

"Sure." Barrett smiled.

He watched as Walton ducked downstairs. Then he counted to one hundred very slowly. All around him, the stillness of the night lay unbroken.

By the time Walton returned to fetch him, Barrett was gone.

Deduction

"H-HELLO?"

"Stroud. It's Barrett."

"*Father* Barrett? What—"

"Sorry to bother you but I need the address of Max Simpson, the Spirit Ranch caretaker."

"Why?"

"His mother's family reached out to me. They're estranged and don't have his contact info but they know he's in Fulton. So they contacted me. I have grave news for him."

"O…kay. Sure. Hang on a sec."

Barrett waited.

"Okay." Stroud returned with a rustling of papers. "He owns property out in the ALR. Has a mobile home. It's 4286 Squamish Road. That's out by…"

"I know where it is. Thanks."

IT WAS the car that should have tipped him off right away. Of course, Max had done a nice soft shoe about being a hard-working, single guy who kept track of his pennies and, gosh, doesn't everyone have a special hobby they just love? Mine is cars, boss, and here I've managed to afford a sports coupe worth almost a quarter million on a caretaker's salary.

Also his sudden departure the day he and Gavin went down to examine the backpack and shoes. And his vagueness about details, where and when things happened. The Chinese girl had said he'd taken Sabrina's shoes. *To no doubt plant them in order to deflect suspicion from himself.* It was all starting to make sense now.

From the look of it, Max was doing booming business in the child trafficking circuit. He'd had five kids— four, after Jason Joe escaped, his lungs full of concrete sealant. No doubt, they all showed traces in their systems from being chained down there for weeks on end. Max cast his net wide from the look of things. Only two of the kids were locals. From the dress and ethnicity of the other two, Barrett assumed they were from out of town.

He guided the Hyundai along the highway outside of town to the turn-off that led to the provincial park and the agricultural land reserve.

Max lived out a distance. The access road off the highway was serviceable, but in poor repair. Cracks zig-zagged along sections of the shoulder and the ever-present potholes, as perennial as dandelions in rural BC, pockmarked the road like asphalt acne. A worn road sign appeared in the headlights, announcing the risk of fire hazard as moderate. Another mentioned a diner ahead, but had the word CLOSED spray-painted across it. Signs of decay from the dying tourist industry were everywhere.

Squamish Road was ahead, a right turn off of the access road. Barrett took the turn. The paved part of the road ran for one hundred yards before softening into sand and gravel. He downshifted and was surprised that it took him over a mile to come across the first property.

This section of the ALR must be huge, he thought. Any man longing for privacy for his nefarious business could do a lot worse than settle here. Barrett passed two more driveways before finding one that was numbered. 1148. Simpson's was 4286. Barrett settled in for a long journey.

The properties were miles apart, some intercut by boundary fencing or separated by access roads like the one he passed immediately before arriving at the foot of a long driveway that ended at a gleaming Lamborghini sports coup parked in the lights of a mobile home. Barrett took note of it, did a U-turn and drove back to the access road. When he reached it, he took a right and followed it up along the boundary line of Simpson's fenced property. Barrett drove in a mile, parked and approached the fence, his cellphone flashlight switched on.

New fencing. He could tell by the paleness of the posts. There would have been considerable outlay for this set-up. Four-foot-tall posts were set at a distance of ten feet apart connected by three tiers of smooth wire. *Electrified?* Barrett bent to examine the tiny electronic module above the middle wire on the nearest post and smirked. *Not electrified,* he thought. *Alarmed.*

He returned to the Hyundai. Getting in, he switched on the ignition and drove nose-first to within five feet of the fence before getting out and rummaging in the trunk for jumper cables.

In his time as a cop, he had learned many things. How to pick a lock, how to rough someone up without leaving bruises, how to get somebody to confess without realizing they'd done so until they'd already spoken. None of these tricks were taught in police academy. Nor was the one he was about to use.

Barrett popped his hood and attached one end of the jumper cables to his battery's posts. Then he left the others on the ground before slipping behind the wheel and switching on the ignition. Once exhaust was pulsing from the muffler, Barrett alighted, grabbed up the positive and negative cable clamps, and clipped them both to the middle fence wire at the same time. The current already running through the fence wires overloaded and the surveillance net died in a cloud of hissing sparks.

Barrett unclamped his battery, re-buttoned the hood, and parked his car on the road, its nose pointing toward town. Then he slipped through the fence wire and began crossing the forest in the direction of Simpson's mobile. He had been traveling less than a minute when the air was split by the sound of a scream.

En Media Res

BARRETT PAUSED AND LISTENED.

It was a woman's voice. No doubt about it. But there was something else, something eerily upsetting. Something familiar that he couldn't put his finger on... Then he remembered.

His cousin Carolyn, who he saw every Christmas and summer, used to make a noise at the same pitch when she dove off the rocks into the lake at the summer cottage. It was a teenage girl noise, one he remembered well. It was one Carolyn no longer made as she grew up and her voice deepened and the teenage girl sounds were replaced by those of a mature woman.

When the sound came again, Barrett was sure of it. The person screaming was a girl. A teenager. Perhaps fourteen. And now he had a fix on her location. He bent his steps in that direction.

Moonlight. Shadows. He was running between trees, alternating his attention from the ground before him to the terrain around. He fought down an image of his cousin Carolyn when the shriek came again, this time accompanied by another sound. Barrett at first thought it might be some kind of insect with a repetitive buzzing. But it soon sharpened into a *swish* of air that sounded like a hiss, ending in a bright *snap!* Like a…

Like a bullwhip.

Hiss…snap!…then the scream. Barrett saw the shapes ahead: the girlish silhouette of someone tied to a tree, an arm raised and visible briefly in the moonlight before plunging forward into shadow, where the hiss-snap-scream began afresh.

Max, his back to Barrett, stood with legs spread. In the moonlight, the naked girl was visible where Simpson had tied her to the trunk of a fat oak. Revulsion swept through Barrett like an ocean tide. What sort of mind would strip a teenage girl, tie her to a tree and whip her?

For that was what Max Simpson was doing. Calmly and methodically, stripped to the waist, his back and torso moiled in sweat, he was flinging forward the bull-whip before taking a breath and drawing it back in great, heaving movements of his shoulders and arms. Then he curled over backwards again, like a discus athlete preparing to spin before throwing his torso forward and casting the whip into shadows to connect with its target. He grunted with each impact.

"You're going to taste this pain," Simpson was saying. "Drink it in deep and good so when the pleasure comes you'll appreciate it, see?"

Barrett crept closer.

The girl was terrified; he could feel the fear radiating from her even at this distance. Apprehension melts into fear, which hardens into terror. People who have ridden the fear merry-go-round past the point of no return reach a point of demoralization where movement becomes impossible to achieve deer-in-the-headlight status. This girl had held still in the hope the stinging lash of Simpson's whip would go away, Now she was bathed in it.

He crept closer, and still closer.

Simpson was enjoying himself, revelling in the theatre of pain. Barrett knew the signs. Simpson was drunk with the drama of inflicting and withholding both agony and respite from it. Here was a sadist in full glory —a man so possessed by ego that his identity has become submerged in the heat of his own flaming lust. Men lust for many things, Barrett knew. And pursuing those lusts change them. As Simpson's had changed him.

Barrett was within a few meters now and still the caretaker had not turned. The whip came back and flew forward, stinging the girl one last time before Barrett launched, hurtling through the remaining foliage, raising a roar of leaves and then clearing the ground between him and Simpson at a dead run. The caretaker had heard and turned, was moving to realign his stance when Barrett shoulder-tackled him. Simpson crashed to the ground beneath the priest's weight, landing with a grunt. He struggled, allowing Barrett to shift and land the first punch.

Simpson was strong, and obviously had some kind of fight training. He bridged beneath Barrett's body and shook him off. Then he was rolling and rising to one knee. Barrett pushed himself into push-up position, placed one foot in the ready-set position and lunged forward before Simpson could rise. Barrett came down on top again. Before Simpson could move, he reared up, raised an arm and smashed his elbow down as hard as he could into the mouth below him.

It hit like an electric shock. Once the elbow

connected, went down (and in), Simpson convulsed like an electric eel discharging or a man spasming in orgasm. The entire quake rattled Barrett, too. He rolled off of Simpson's pulsing body, rose to his feet, and waited.

Despite his facial wound, Simpson was scrabbling at the ground beneath him, rolling himself over and trying to stand—

Barrett lashed out in a vicious kick, the toe-cap of one shoe connecting with Simpson's ribs at high velocity. The caretaker screeched and collapsed. And when he did, Barrett jumped and landed with the entire weight of both feet on the back of Simpson's hand, shattering every bone in it. Simpson whimpered, went into shock, and passed out.

Barrett made sure he was out, then approached the tree, untied the girl and wrapped his jacket around her shoulders.

"What's your name?" he asked gently.

"Cynthia Howard. From Connecticut. Where is this?"

"You're in British Columbia. Vancouver Island, to be exact. I'm guessing you were kidnapped and brought here?"

She was nodding.

"I'm sorry." Barrett patted her shoulder. "You alone here? Yes? Just you and him? Okay." He pointed. "If you follow that orange glow, you'll come to the Spirit Ranch housing development. There's a policeman there named Lewis. Find him. Tell him I sent you. My name is Father Barrett. He'll help."

The woman pulled the coat tight around her shoulders. "Thank you, father." She looked down at Simpson. "And what about him?"

"He and I will finish our chat when he comes around." Barrett smiled. "You'd best be on your way, Ms. Howard. Be safe and have a good evening."

Drag

WHEN SIMPSON CAME TO, he was facing a modest log fire Barrett had built inside the stone circle in the double-wide's yard. He felt something pressing his back but overbalanced when he tried to lean forward. That's when he realized he was wrapped in chain, his arms tight against his sides, his ankles also secured by a wrapped length of chain.

Barrett was sitting on a log on the other side of the fire, an open bottle of brandy on his knee from which he took periodic sips as he stared into the flames. He looked up when Simpson stirred.

"The way this usually begins is with an incantation. I'll start you out. *Forgive me father, for I have sinned.'* That's the formulation. Try it."

Simpson's hand, ribs and mouth shrieked in pain. He waggled his jaw from side to side. He could speak, if he was careful of his broken teeth. But he could not enunciate well. "For—gih me, fatha. Fo' ah haf snnnd."

Barrett gestured with the bottle of brandy he had taken from the kitchen cabinet. "That car should have tipped me off right away. It's worth a quarter-million dollars. No way a nice, hard-working guy like you could have afforded it. Even if you didn't eat and did all your own laundry between the ages of ten and forty-six. No, you're into something nefarious. Downright evil." Barrett's glare bored into his skull. "You're the bagman for the child traffickers. Their Krampus. Their Pied Piper. You snatch the kiddies and sell them to…"

Simpson shook his head. Firmly, even though it smarted. He glared defiantly back, water rimming his eyes.

At this, Barrett smiled and reached into his jacket. Simpson's eyes widened when he drew it back. "That's right," Barrett said. "I checked in your medicine cabinet. Quite a pharmacopeia you keep! Including this Dilaudid. Man, that stuff's hard to score. And for good reason. It's powerful enough to do away with every ache and pain you're experiencing right now. Because I'm not calling the ambulance until you answer all my questions. The moment you have, you get this…and a nice comfy wait for the ambulance in nice warm, fuzzy narcotic cocoon. So what do you say? Play ball with me?"

"Yah." Simpson winced at the way his jaw clicked.

"Okay. So." Barrett toasted him, took a sip of brandy, and asked: "Who you in with?"

Simpson breathed raggedly through his busted mouth and teeth, then began speaking in a broken whisper.

"Had…debt. Bad debt. Could nah pay. Frien' of a frien'. Loaner. Money at interes'. Turns out. Vietnamese. Crim-mi-mal gang. Nanaimo. Very, very dan-ger-ous."

"Okay. So you were into the shylocks. Which was worse than your credit card bills. So they started you small, right? Doing what? Driving bigshots around?

Collecting protection money?" He shuddered saying this, remembering Mr. Yi's special soup. "Making you work off your debt?"

"They di'. Yah. Like tha'. Then found out. How much. Money. Could make! Paid debt. Wen' inna business with 'em."

"Kidnapping kids."

"Selling drugs a'them a' firs'. But, yeah. Even'ually."

Barrett drew in a deep breath to ask for more but then Simpson was talking on his own.

"Star'ed drivin'. Goin' for drives. Down islan'. Nanaimo. Parksville. Inna' the Valley. Every few month. Go see malls. Si' ou'side high schools. Cruise aroun'. Lookin' for girls, mos'ly. Cus'omers pay top dollar for tha'. So I fin' 'em. Pull ovah. Show 'em the cah. Ge' chatty."

"And then you'd pull them in. Right?" Barrett took a long hard swig of brandy without releasing Simpson from his glare. "Go out on your little child-finding expeditions, locate and engage one before abducting them. What did you use? Chloroform? Quaaludes? Something mixed into a soft drink or other beverage?"

"A spray." Simpson's eyes slid toward the pill in Barrett's fingers as he spoke. "They provided. Dunno' wha's in i'. And I have-a be careful wi' the win', and like tha'. But one blas' of this. Inna face. A' close range? Ligh's ou'."

Simpson paused and considered.

"Make 'en thousand per kid each." He turned his imploring gaze to Barrett. "C'n I ha' pill?"

"Not yet." Barrett smiled and let the thing roll into his hand. "So you get ten grand per child that you abduct and hand over to this Vietnamese gang in Nanaimo. You got names?"

"On my cell." Simpson grimaced with the effort to locate and pat his pocket. "Name o' Tranh."

"Okay."

"Say. Any chan' you coul' un'ie me for a bi'?"

"No. So your contact in Nanaimo is a Vietnamese gang member named Tranh whose contact info is on your cellphone." Barrett came around, reached into Simpson's pocket and produced his Android. It wasn't password protected, Barrett thumbed to Tranh's page in the contact files. "This him?" Barrett held up the number. Simpson nodded.

And Barrett smiled.

"Thank you, Mr. Simpson. You have been very helpful. Absolutely first rate. No ifs, ands, or buts. I appreciate your cooperation. And your frankness. It's going to make resolving this whole business a whole lot easier once it goes to court."

"Will I ge' wi'ness pro'ection, you think?"

"Witness protection? No. I should think not." Barrett slid the phone into a coat pocket. "No, you won't need witness protection. Either before or during the trial. You're not going to be in any danger from them at all."

"Why?"

"Because you'll be dead, of course." Barrett blinked. "You don't think I intend to let you live given everything you've done to all these kids, do you? Fuck no, amigo. Your goose is cooked. Deep fried. Oven roasted. And very well done. It's time for you to face your final judgment, son. To reap the rewards of all your hard work."

Barrett reached into his pocket, produced the keys to Simpson's Lamborghini, and shook them.

"Wha' ah' you do'in w—"

"What am I doing with these?" Barrett chuckled. "Good question, me bucko."

Barrett rose slowly and walked toward Simpson, continuing until he had walked past him. Simpson turned his head to follow, but Barrett soon wandered out of sight. Simpson cursed. His head would only turn so far. But it turned far enough to see that Barrett had chained him and then leaned him up against a tree stump, where he now suffered.

An interminable period passed before he heard something. It was one of the doors on the Lambo. Then he heard the muffled blast of the car's engine being started, the *crump* of a gear shifting and then the long, slow purr of the engine in motion. Soon he heard tires crunching close behind him. Then the car switched off and Barrett was doing something that involved more chains. Or so he thought.

Barrett returned to the fire, crossed to his place and picked up the brandy bottle.

"Here's the thing, Max," he said, taking a swig. "What you've done is not just wrong. And not just illegal. It's evil, in the purest sense of the word. Honest-to-God, one hundred percent, USDA-approved evil. And that takes some doing."

"I...look. Father. I go' issues..."

"Issues? I'll say!" Barrett sipped. "What kind of sick motherfucker decides to make kidnapping innocent children his life's work?"

"No! The ca'! The Lambo! Tha's mah life's work!"

"Ah. Here we see the pitfalls of secular philosophy at work. Is your life's work the thing to which you aspire? Or is it the thing you're actually *doing?* See, I would argue the latter. Know why?"

"The ca'! The ca'!"

Barrett ignored him. "The reason, Max, is simple. It's because, in this life, we become what we do. No, really.

We do. The same holds true for our treatment of people. Ever notice how, the more you treat someone badly, the less you care about them? And it works in reverse. Practice love with people and soon you'll find yourself caring about them more." Barrett shrugged. "That's something I'm learning. Fake it 'til you make it.'"

"You don' li' people?" Max seemed momentarily stunned.

"Not really." Barrett stared morosely into the fire. "My father was an awful man. Involved in organized crime. I saw him kill another man when I was just a boy. And I saw him torture another one when I was a little older. My father looked with contempt upon the world because he treated others with contempt. They were just pawns to be bullied and pushed around to get what he wanted."

"And you' just like him!"

"Me? Just like him?" Barrett frowned. "There may be something to that. A chip off the old block, as they say. Could be. Could be. But I think the difference is both in trajectory and point of departure. He started as a hood. I started as a priest. He hated people and wanted to torture them. I hated them and wanted forgiveness for it."

"So le' me go!" Simpson shook his chains.

"Forgiveness for *me*. Not you. It's not my place to judge or forgive you. That's God's place." Barrett took a long swallow of brandy and studied the label, considering. "And I don't envy God that task. You, even less. Because you're going to be forced to face each and every incident involving yourself and a child. You'll be made to relive the pain you inflicted on that child, and everything that comes after. Not sure what kind of person *buys* a child, but I'm guessing not the kind who's particularly interested in that child's welfare. No, they probably view the investment as disposable. A luxury status item, like a car or a yacht or a frigging grand piano."

Barrett dashed the bottle into the fire, causing it to shatter. The brandy hit the logs and ignited, causing the fire to leap high. Barrett glared down at Simpson through the lunging streamers of flame.

"The children you funnel to your Vietnamese pals probably end up chained in the basements of the wealthy and powerful worldwide. Sheikhs and princes and the CEOs of multinational corporations. I'm guessing their lives aren't too pleasant, what with forced captivity, endless terror, and periodic sexual molestation. You're going to see what that's all like. You're going to experience it."

"You're gonna' sell me?"

"Nah." Barrett walked behind Simpson, who heard a dim *clank* before Barrett returned holding a length of stout chain in his fist. "I can't imagine anyone wanting to buy you."

Barrett dropped the chain, grasped Simpson by the shoulders, and hauled him away from the tree stump. When he let go, the caretaker fell to one side, chained and curled on the ground like a shrimp.

"No," Barrett said conversationally, dropping to his knees and taking up the chain. "It's God who will make you relive all that stuff. God who will grant you the grace to see exactly how much evil you've inflicted in the world. You deserve to know."

Simpson felt something at his back. Barrett was twisting the chain he held in amongst the chains that bound him. Barrett finished looping them together and then secured them with one of the padlocks he'd found in Simpson's workshop.

"So." Barrett stood. "I'm not here to judge you. Or condemn you. But I am here to bring you before the Judge of the World for your sins. I am prepared to hear your confession and offer absolution to you before you go."

"Absolution? No, father. I'd rather stand and be judged."

"Suit yourself."

Barrett turned and marched to the Lamborghini. Ducking inside, he took his place behind the wheel and started the car, the engine drowning out Simpson's screams. Barrett put the car in gear and it lurched into motion, stalling briefly as it encountered then accepted Simpson's weight as part of its burden. Barrett put the car in second and began driving down the driveway, turning left as he hit the road. He paused briefly, listening. Simpson's screams had become a series of ragged whimpers, broken by sobs. Even this short drag down his own driveway would have been enough to knock the fight out of him. But it was nothing compared to what lay ahead. Simpson's nearest neighbor was two miles away. Barrett pressed the accelerator…

Simpson's scream coincided with the roar of the engine and continued through first gear. It died by the time Barrett found second. By the time he'd reached third gear, Simpson was making no sound.

None at all.

Resolution

BARRETT WAS STANDING in the hospital ambulance bay smoking a cigarette when Lewis pulled up in his patrol car. The Mountie looked exhausted but happy as he stepped out and locked the car behind him. He wandered over to Barrett with a tired smile in place.

"How are things?" asked Barrett casually.

"Good." Lewis sighed as he stepped up beside the priest. They stared out at the parking lot together. "Child welfare services arrived a few hours back. They're getting the identity of those kids and notifying their families. Jason Joe regained consciousness this morning. He and Sabrina are back with the tribe now."

"I bet the Chief is relieved."

"He is." Lewis smiled. "They're apparently going to have a big do at their longhouse tomorrow night. We're invited. A welcome back party, I suppose. There will probably be prayers and such. And a banquet. The tribes like their banquets."

"I'll bring the wine."

"They don't drink in the longhouse, padre. You should know that."

"Of course." Barrett produced his cigarettes and lit a fresh one off the stub of his last. "So the kids are alright."

"They are. Nanaimo joint task force moved in on that Vietnamese gang last night. Arrested a half-dozen guys, including that guy Tranh. Two of them rolled over on the rest. They admitted to child trafficking. And they gave us the name of their local source. Are you ready for this?" Lewis was watching Barrett carefully now.

"Who is it?" Barrett took a deep drag off his cigarette and waited.

Lewis' gaze lingered on him for an impossibly long moment before he resumed. "Turns out our kidnapper was none other than Max Simpson."

"Max? You mean the caretaker?" Barrett affected surprise. "No kidding. Well, I suppose that explains his expensive taste in cars..."

"Mm." Lewis squinted at Barrett one final moment before returning his attention to the lot. "Apparently, Simpson owed them money. They loan-sharked him into taking the job and he ended up getting a taste for it. He supplied them with more kids than they needed on a regular basis. Made quite a pile of dough. But he still fell afoul of them."

"How so?"

"We found his body on a logging road in the ALR. Somebody had chained him to the back of his Lamborghini and taken him for a drag." Lewis made a disgusted sound in the back of his throat. "Got torn to ribbons on the rocks. There wasn't much of him left. It looks like a gang related revenge killing."

Barrett swallowed. "God," he whispered quietly. And left it at that.

They were still standing there when Stroud pulled up in his Lincoln. The attorney parked and approached them, his ever-present briefcase dangling from his right wrist as he checked the watch on his left.

"Sergeant. Father." Stroud sighed. "I guess this is it."

Barrett nodded. "He's fading fast, counsellor."

"Okay," Stroud said. "We'd better get up there."

They entered the hospital's emergency waiting room, walking past the charge nurse to the elevators. They rose to the otherwise deserted floor of the hospice wing, where a cluster of hospice workers and a doctor clustered around the nurses' station.

"Father Barrett." The doctor stepped forward. "A word?"

"Sure." Barrett stepped aside to talk to the doctor as Lewis and Stroud conferred by the door to McLellan's room. "How is he?"

"He's fading." The doctor looked grim. "He actually flatlined for a while early this morning, around two o'clock. But he came back. He's in and out of consciousness. And when he's awake, it's at varying levels of coherence."

"Hm. Okay."

"I understand you resigned as his spiritual advisor." The doctor looked puzzled. "Is that correct?"

"Yeah, but… Under the circumstances, I figured I'd show up."

"Thank you." The doctor sighed. "It will ease his transition. I appreciate it."

Lewis was beckoning. Barrett thanked the doctor and followed Lewis and Stroud into McLellan's room.

He's not long for it now, Barrett thought, examining the shrunken figure in the hospital bed. McLellan had lost fifty pounds. His face was drawn and puckered and his skin held a greyish tone. Death was very close. Barrett knew the signs.

Sitting beside the bed in a chair and holding McLellan's hand was his eldest son Tristan. Tears stood in his eyes. Barrett moved to stand behind him and laid a hand on his shoulder.

"How you doing, Tristan?" he asked.

The young man trembled where he sat. Barrett marvelled at the broadness of Tristan's shoulders, of the prodigious height of the man. McLellan was little taller than Barrett's five-nine. How he had produced such a Sasquatch was beyond the priest. He wondered if the other brother was just as big.

"No sign of Mark?" Stroud asked.

"No!" Tristan's sadness became tearful rage. "Why would he come? He's been gone for decades. Never cared a rip about dad or the family. Even when he was still living with us, he was a problem! Stealing stuff. Breaking things. No, he's not here and thank God for that."

"You're just h...*happy*. To be the sole *heir!*" McLellan sputtered from his prone position. "Like you ever..." He broke off in a spasm of coughing before finishing. "Like you ever *cared* about me! Beyond the money!"

"Oh, dad. Don't talk about that now." Tristan squeezed his hand. Barrett thought he detected a note of insincerity in the move.

Stroud opened his briefcase. "As you requested, Mr. McLellan, I have a final version of your Last Will and Testament. All the changes you requested have been made."

Barrett wondered what sort of last-minute adjustments McLellan had made regarding his financial posterity. He felt momentarily sorry for Tristan—spoiled, naïve, angry Tristan. Staring ruin in the face had to hurt in one's mid-forties after a life of privilege and ease. But here he was, hanging onto the inheritance roller-coaster for one last whirl down the track of his father's whims.

Stroud laid the document on the wheeled table used for food and drink service and pushed it to McLellan's bed. The aged mogul grasped feebly for it, fingers catching the table's edge and crimping the corners of a few pages before Stroud stepped in to handle it for him.

"Allow me." The attorney cleared his throat and licked a thumb to turn pages. "We've consolidated your real estate holdings into a blind trust. That should generate interest for your second-level beneficiaries, the directors and managers of your various ventures. Their pay-out will occur over a three-year period, at which point the trust will be converted…as we see here."

Stroud flipped a page and reached for a pen in his jacket pocket.

"We'll need your initials for this amendment here. This is a hold-harmless clause for your beneficiaries in the event any of your pending litigation goes against the estate. The blind trust will be exempt. So your primary assets will be targeted as compensatory."

"What 'primary assets'?" demanded Tristan. "Are we talking the house?"

Stroud nodded. "Yes, Tristan. Mr. McLellan's home, his land holdings, his assets including vehicles, art objects, antiques…"

"Well, is there going to be anything left for *me?*" Tristan's voice cracked on the last word.

As he spoke, Walton entered the room and went directly to Lewis. Barrett noted urgency in the Conservation officer's steps. He drew out a folded piece of paper, which he opened and showed to Lewis. McLellan, meanwhile, was gesturing with the pen Stroud had provided as he spoke.

"Tristan, listen. This money isn't just for you. I have a community—hell, a *town*—to think of. You imagine Fulton would be what it is without me?"

"Of course not, dad."

McLellan scrawled his initials on the page. "We've amended the will based on the outcome of my lawsuit with those occult freaks in the Black Star Temple. Anton here tells me chances are excellent they'll settle out of court in order to avoid an investigation by Revenue Canada. So..."

"Um." Lewis stepped forward, the paper Walton had given him in hand. "Mr. McLellan, I have some news." He unfolded the paper and stared down at it. "We just received notification that any litigation related to Spirit Ranch Estates has been stayed by order of the Crown."

"What?" Stroud frowned, reaching. "Let me see that..."

Lewis handed it over. Stroud bent, squinting at the notice on official government letterhead. He read a few lines before looking up in disbelief.

"Archaeological findings? What the hell is this?"

"We had a group out here from Indigenous Affairs and the University of Victoria last week," Walton said. "They were excavating on the boundary line between the Spirit Ranch and the First Nations reserve. The results of their investigation have confirmed the presence of First Nations burial sites on the land. Some going back hundreds of years."

McLellan's head drooped. The pen fell from his fingers.

"Basically, the Crown has seized Spirit Ranch estates." Walton shrugged. "It's property of the Government of Canada at this point. In all likelihood, it will be ceded back to the tribe as a gesture of reconciliation."

"What about our investment?" thundered Tristan.

Walton shrugged. "Easy come, easy go," he said.

Stroud laid the letter on the table beside McLellan's will. "I'm sorry, Arnold," he said softly. "This supersedes any prior claims or contracts. A Crown order is, well..."

McLellan suddenly looked very weak, as if he were just holding onto life by the slimmest thread. The life was draining out of him. Barrett knew the signs.

"How the hell..." McLellan was shaking his head. "We surveyed that site carefully. Found no traces of burial grounds. So how the hell did they get it into their heads to come back with archaeologists? What possessed them to do that?"

"*I* called them."

As one, the group turned to the door.

Squatch stood there. Bearded, his hair matted with oil and dirt, his sturdy clothes torn and the ever-present duffel bag over his shoulder, he glared at McLellan and Tristan with real rage.

"Mark?" Tristan half rose. "What..."

"Oh, Jesus," muttered Lewis. "Squatch is McLellan's lost son, Mark."

"Wow," said Walton.

Thy weird be done, thought Barrett, and crossed himself.

"You're *done!*" Tristan was on his feet, one hand clenched in a fist, the other pointing at Mark. "You're *out!* You haven't been a part of this family for decades! Now you have the nerve to show up at the last minute, just as dad is dying, to get your piece of the pie? Not happening!"

Mark smiled. "You think I'd be living in the woods

all these years if I gave a shit about your precious pie, Tristan? Anyway, sounds like dad didn't leave much for you. What there is, you're welcome to." He turned to Lewis. "I've spent years searching the site for artifacts. It's been slow going. I work mostly after dark. But I finally found enough stuff to send a package to Heritage Canada. They contacted Indigenous Affairs. And they've done the right thing."

"Justice served," said Lewis with a smile.

"That's fine! That's fine!" Tristan flipped a hand. "So Spirit Ranch is lost. The rest is tied up in a trust to benefit dad's employees. I'll be fine with the house. I'll sell it and be a rich man."

McLellan's grasped Tristan's hand. "Son," he said quietly. "I hate to say it, but... You won't."

Tristan's face grew pale. "What are you saying?" he whispered.

"I'm sorry, Tristan. But I took out a third mortgage on the place. Figured to pay it off with the proceeds of the development, but..."

"But what?"

"I'm afraid the bank owns it, son." He smiled apologetically. "Can you forgive me?"

Tristan struggled to answer his father, his shock palpable. McLellan waited patiently. And he was still waiting when his eyes glazed over and the heart monitor flat-lined.

"He's gone," Barrett said quietly. He stepped over and closed McLellan's eyes. Then he began delivering Last Rites.

A Look at Book Three:
ARCHBISHOP'S CONFESSION

A COMBINATION OF SINISTER BLEAKNESS AND EVER-PRESENT DANGER—FATHER BARRETT IS BACK FOR BOOK THREE IN THIS SINISTER MYSTERY SERIES.

Ex-Vatican investigator Father Michael Barrett has been ordered to attend Alcoholics Anonymous by his superior, Archbishop Crowe. Coinciding with a surge in violent street crime and the appearance of a strange newcomer among the local homeless population called the Garbage Messiah, Barrett's attendance at AA leads to him forming a bond with Anglican minister Kelly Ward—an ex-infantry officer still haunted by her tour of duty in Afghanistan.

Thus, when Barrett's deacon goes missing and local crimes escalate to stabbings and shootings that sideline law enforcement, Barrett and Ward decide to join forces.

Two priests, an ex-cop and an ex-soldier, plunge into a maelstrom of evil and criminal violence—pulling no punches in their effort to find a missing deacon, take down the Garbage Messiah and spare small-town Fulton from becoming a war zone.

AVAILABLE OCTOBER 2022

About the Author

Jamie Mason is the author of several science fiction novels and thrillers. Born in Montreal, he attended the University of Arizona and Chapman University. After a decade spent teaching in the southwest, he returned to Canada in 2005. He has worked variously as a think-tank analyst, a business manager, a professional musician and a private investigator. Now semi-retired and living in the woods of Vancouver Island, he devotes his time to writing and savoring the vanishing Canadian wilderness.